MAKING WAVES

D1324806

Also by Bisto Award Winning Author
Jane Mitchell

When Stars Stop Spinning
Different Lives
Olivia's Collection

Published by Poolbeg

JANE MITCHELL

MAKING WAVES

POOLBEG

Published 1998 by
Poolbeg Press Ltd,
123 Baldoyle Industrial Estate,
Dublin 13, Ireland

© Jane Mitchell 1998

The moral right of the author has been asserted.

The Arts Council
An Chomhairle Ealaíon

A catalogue record for this book is available from the British Library.

ISBN 1 85371 828 9

Cover illustration by Daivd Axtell
Cover design by Poolbeg Group Services Ltd
Set by Poolbeg Group Services Ltd in Goudy 10.5/14
Printed and bound in Great Britain by
Cox & Wyman Ltd, Reading, Berkshire.

With thanks to Paul
for the title

Chapter 1

Bleep . . . bleep . . . bleep . . .

Five am. November.

The timer on her watch pipped insistently, dragging Ciara Vaughan from a blissful world of deep dreams into a cold, dark dawn. She yawned sleepily and stretched. God, bed was great. She was just so comfortable that no matter how she moved or what position she adopted, she felt she could have stayed like that forever. Drifting deliciously between sleeping and wakefulness, it was as though she were floating on air. She was completely burrowed beneath her duvet, the deep folds of it wrapped around her like a second skin.

Bleep . . . bleep . . . bleep . . .

Damn. There was her watch again. Without opening her eyes, Ciara groped for her wrist and pressed the button on the side of the watch. She turned over in the bed, snuffling around underneath the covers, seeking the last spot she'd made warm.

But she couldn't find just the right place for her arms and legs to go.

1

There was this little flurry of cold air that rushed in and tickled her elbow.

Then her knee found an icy patch that made her whole leg go shivery. Whenever her bare toes touched cold sheets, she pulled back, screwing up her nose and grunting with dislike.

Her cosy sleepiness was rapidly dissolving.

The bed wasn't a fluffy, warm cloud any more. It was lumpy and it squeaked as she moved around.

And there was a cold front rapidly approaching, resulting in isolated frosts and gale warnings.

She was going to sneeze.

It was no use.

She was awake now and knew she wouldn't get back to sleep. Grumpily, Ciara poked her nose out into the bedroom and sniffed the air. God, it was *cold*. How was she going to get up and move around in that temperature? She sleepily opened her eyes and peeked round her bedroom. It was still dark.

A door across the landing opened softly and a slice of gold from the hall light squeezed through the gap at the bottom of Ciara's door. The sound of creaking floorboards approached her room. A burglar wouldn't get far in their house, Ciara thought as she listened until the floorboard two steps from her door groaned in the effort of supporting her father. Not that he needed great support – he wasn't a ten-ton elephant or anything. She waited. One, two seconds and he'd knock.

There was a gentle knock and the door opened.

"Ciara. Sorcha. Rise and shine, girls. I'm taking the car out and I want you both in it in ten minutes."

"Morning, Dad," Ciara muttered.

He didn't exactly sound full of the joys of spring either, Ciara decided. After all, five-fifteen isn't a natural time for anyone to have to force their body into action.

Ciara's older sister Sorcha fervently believed that the typical human body, if left to its own devices without the interference of alarm-clocks or fathers, isn't normally ready for activity until at least eleven o'clock in the morning. "It's not natural to disturb a person from their sleep. It can lead to all sorts of problems," she'd regularly state. "The human system should be left to rouse itself passively."

Sorcha was living proof of her own theory, staying on in bed until midday whenever possible, which wasn't very often as she was usually unceremoniously hauled out of the bed three mornings a week at five-fifteen am. "This is damaging my circadian rhythm," she'd argue.

Ciara lifted her head as her father closed the door on his way out. She peered through the gloom to her sister's bed. Sorcha was a motionless mound beneath a tangle of covers on the other side of the room. Whatever about Ciara trying to get roused early, Sorcha was ten times worse. Ciara reached beneath her bed, feeling around for something suitable to throw at her sister. She picked up her runner and flung it across the room where it walloped against the radiator, the hollow clanging noise right against Sorcha's ear.

3

"What was that?" Sorcha grumbled groggily, startled by the noise. Another dent in your circadian rhythm, Ciara thought. "Get up," Ciara told her, clambering out of bed herself and quickly pulling on her track suit. It was all go, no time to spare. Lacing up one runner, she hopped across and retrieved the other from beneath Sorcha's bed and gave Sorcha an extra poke for good measure. Without a word, Sorcha rolled over and landed with a thud on the floor, taking her duvet with her. By the time Ciara was ready to go downstairs, Sorcha was crawling out of her burrow.

Ciara's kit-bag was ready packed in the hall. Her watch began bleeping again. It was now five-twenty-five am. Shift your butt, Ciara, she told herself.

By the time she grabbed her bag and ran out the front door, her father had reversed the car out of the driveway and was scraping the frost from the windows. The exhaust pumped clouds of steam into the morning darkness – eerie clouds of white mist. Ciara opened the passenger door and sat in, hunching herself over to keep a little warmth in her body. She was sleepy from bed and hoped that if she kept herself scrunched up enough, her body wouldn't notice that she wasn't still there.

Her father sat into the driver's seat just as Sorcha pulled the front door behind her and joined them. Five-thirty-two and they set out for the ten-minute drive to the swimming-pool.

The roads were empty of traffic. Apart from the occasional lone worker on the way to an early shift, the dark streets were deserted.

They were silent in the car, each of them enveloped in a shroud of sleepiness. Sorcha had dozed off in the back seat, her jaw dropping open. Ciara stared stupidly ahead of her until her eyes watered and she blinked several times and yawned.

"What are you working on this morning?" Her father's voice broke the silence.

Ciara yawned again. "I don't know. I only hope it's not sprint swimming. I don't think I could handle that this morning. I'm sorry now I stayed up for that stupid film last night. It wasn't worth it. It wasn't over until nine-thirty."

They pulled into the carpark of the swimming pool. Two or three cars were there already. The fluorescent lights of the reception area looked harsh in the blackness of the morning. Their father turned the car and stopped.

"I'll pick you up at seven-forty-five," he said as Ciara grabbed her kit-bag and hopped out.

She nodded in reply and then knocked on the back window. Sorcha emerged, zombie-like, and followed Ciara through the double doors into the pool.

The strong smell of chlorine hit them full force as they opened the door. Ciara loved the smell. It reminded her of the excitement of swimming, the buzz she got from the whole deal. The odour was distinctive and unique. It spoke of galas and churning water and the thrill of competition. It injected energy into her step immediately and she perked up, sleepiness forgotten in anticipation of the clear, blue water.

"I hate the whiff of the pool as soon as you walk in

the door," Sorcha commented. "It gets under your fingernails and seeps into your skin and clings to every hair. It stays with you all day and you go round the place smelling like a human chemistry lab."

Ever since the girls were tiny, they had been swimming. Their father was passionate about the sport and had swum for Ireland when he had been in college. When Sorcha was born, he had brought her to the pool and released her in the deep end as soon as she had had all her vaccinations, him treading water next to her, lifting her out every few seconds so she could breathe. Ciara had followed her sister's paddling a year later.

"Children don't ever need to be taught to swim," he'd explained to them when they were older. "It's an instinctive ability that an infant is born with, but they forget it as they get older and need to be taught from scratch. A baby's movement in water echoes the movement in the womb and so, the younger they start, the more intact their memory. Babies will automatically stop breathing when underwater, so they won't drown. I had to watch you both very carefully because you were so tiny that you weren't able to lift your heads to breathe. I'd lift you clear of the water every four or five seconds."

True enough, neither of the girls had any memory of actually learning to swim. They had just always been able to do it, and loved anything to do with water because it felt so comfortable to them. By the time Ciara and Sorcha were two and three years respectively, they were completely independent in their swimming. The depth of the water made no difference because they were so small, they couldn't reach the bottom in the shallow end anyway. It sometimes caused great worry to others on family holidays when these two toddlers would waddle over to whatever pool was near their apartment and plunge in to the deep end while their mum and dad calmly sipped drinks on the poolside. Of course, their parents were always around keeping an eye on them, but they didn't need to be in the water, hovering with floats and rubber rings and armbands. On several occasions, other holidaymakers rushed over to the pool in great panic to fish out what they thought were two drowning children, only to find them bobbing around quite happily.

By the time Sorcha started school, they both wanted to swim more and more. Weekend swimming with Mum and Dad wasn't enough. The mothers-and-toddlers group that Ciara went to while Sorcha was at school was a joke. The other little children screamed and clung to their mothers with fright, while Ciara dived to the bottom of the pool to retrieve coins her mother dropped in for her. When asked what they wanted to do in their free time, the girls would always ask for swimming.

"Please, Mummy, please bring me and Ciara to swimming," Sorcha would beg, always the spokesperson for the two of them.

So they'd joined a club for under-twelves. They were the youngest by about three years and the club insisted that their mother accompany them all the time, but their competitive swimming started from there.

Now, the girls trained hard several mornings a week before school, as well as afternoon training and dry-land weights training to strengthen their muscles. It was a serious business they were into, that demanded a great deal of the family's energy, time and resources. But Ciara wouldn't have it any other way. She loved it. They all did.

As they walked past the pool office now, Martha, the pool attendant, looked up from her desk.

"Morning, Sorcha; morning, Ciara," she said brightly.

"Good morning, Martha," Ciara said.

Sorcha didn't quite seem able to muster the energy to respond to Martha's cheery greeting. They walked on down the corridor to the changing room, which was empty. A few kit-bags and towels were scattered on the benches.

"I think we're late," Sorcha muttered as they peeled off their track suits.

On the poolside, Mark stood in his shorts and poolside shoes, his T-shirt stuck to him from the heat generated by the swimmers and the heated pool. He tapped the face of his watch when Ciara and Sorcha emerged from the changing room.

"Five-forty-five, ladies," he stated flatly, walking over to them. "What do you mean by turning up so late? There's no way I can manage your training if you leave me so short of time. You've missed my pep talk, not to mention most of the warm-up. What happens then? We end up with bad technique and poor stamina, that's what! And when you lose your next race, it'll be 'But

Mark, you're our trainer, why didn't you push us harder?' or 'Mark, that race was the most important one in my *life* and I wasn't ready. Why did you make me swim it?' And it won't be my fault, will it? Get out of my sight! Into the pool – take lane 5. Start off with an 800-metre crawl, breathing on alternate sides, six flutter kicks. Take a fifteen-second break on every hundred and then start working your way through the warm-up programme till six."

There were already several other swimmers in the pool, churning up and down. They were at various stages in the warm-up programme, which was chalked up on a blackboard hanging on the wall. The programme was divided into different distances and strokes. It was intended to be swum without break, except for the ten- or fifteen-second stops usually at the end of every two hundred metres, or eight lengths of the twenty-five-metre pool.

Sorcha and Ciara walked over to their lane without replying. The lane was empty. Nobody by choice would go to a lane against the wall. It cramped your swim too much. Ciara adjusted her hat, pulling it away from her ears.

"Tacky lane," she muttered.

"Tacky coach," Sorcha replied under her breath, grinning at her sister.

"Have a good swim," Ciara called as she dived into the pool. Although the water was warm, the shock of it was cold against her skin. Her arms and legs broke out in goose bumps. The startle of the water made her gasp and

9

surface quickly. The first dive of the morning was the one part of swimming that Ciara disliked, especially on a frosty winter morning when it was still dark outside. She swam quickly, using a short, shallow pull and a fast kick to get her blood moving. She could hear Mark shouting at her from the poolside.

"Reach out, Ciara. Don't hug your arm to your body. Long pulls. Deep kicks."

She ignored him. "Give me a break, Mark," she thought. "That's all very well when you've warmed up, but not until then."

By five past six, Ciara had finished most of the warm-up. The other swimmers had gone on to their individual programmes, while a whole bunch of younger swimmers had arrived to do their training. Two additional coaches had arrived on the poolside to train them and they all stood together in a group, going over their programmes. Mark kept to the senior swimmers and the junior champions. He fine-tuned and built up the swimmers who showed potential, pushing them to the limit all the time. Not that they needed it; most of them pushed themselves harder than he did, arriving to the pool at five-fifteen or five-thirty to squeeze in an extra few minutes of swimming before the formal programme.

Ciara and Sorcha climbed out of the pool, vacating their lane which was immediately filled by masses of young swimmers who dipped and dived in the water like tadpoles before a sharp blow on a whistle from one of the coaches brought them to order.

Mark came over to the two girls, carrying his clipboard.

"OK, we're working on breaststroke this morning. Sorcha, I want you to work on arm action. Take six by 200 metres, giving yourself twenty seconds between hundreds. Work on arm extension, with an early catch point. Arms only on the front length, arms and legs together on the return. Got it? Don't bother timing yourself, concentrate on your technique. I'll come round to you in a few minutes."

"What lane will I take?" Sorcha asked.

"Lane 2. Slot in between Gavin and Niamh."

Sorcha moved off to begin her programme. Mark turned to Ciara. He shrugged.

"What's going on?" he demanded, his voice brittle. Great, here we go. Ciara knew this was coming. From the time she'd walked into the pool, Mark had been warming up for a good old barney with her. She could see it in his expression. He got seriously narked if one of his top swimmers was late for one training session. He was fit to be tied if that swimmer was late for a whole run of training sessions, as had happened to Ciara. He started off with gusto.

"What's with this arriving ten minutes after we've started? If you want to get a reasonable time at the end of the season, you'll have to start getting here before we begin training proper. And I mean twenty minutes or half an hour beforehand, so you get your warm-up done and can get straight into training. You'll also need to start arriving here for morning training at least four times a week – three's just not enough. Not for you. You'll be good, Ciara. No, you'll be great! I know it. But you need to get into the pool more, push yourself on technique and skills."

"How am I supposed to do that?" Ciara asked herself silently. "I live eight miles away. My father has to get up to drive Sorcha and me here. He isn't exactly throwing a party about that. It's the least I can do to be grateful he gets me here at all, not start harping on at him for not getting me here bang on time." Anyway, Mark was rattling on.

"Otherwise you may as well throw in the towel completely and not bother with the senior competitions. You know the opposition's tough. You know your best times are hovering just above the qualifying times for next season's championships. You need to knock a few seconds off most of your events, especially the 400-metre Individual Medley. You're well able to, if you grit your teeth and get down to it. But I can't work you up if you're so late on the few days you do get here, it's impossible. You can't expect me – or yourself – to work miracles."

The 400-metre Individual Medley, or 400 IM as it was usually called, was Ciara's best event. And her favourite. It was a combination of all of the four strokes: breast, backstroke, front crawl and butterfly swum over 400 metres. That meant each of the strokes got 100 metres, or four lengths of a 25-metre pool. Ciara's best two strokes, the breast and the front crawl were the last two strokes swum in the 400 IM which meant that she always made up precious distance and usually triumphed with a medal in the event. But with the way her times were at the moment, she wouldn't be scooping any medals in the IM next season.

Ciara glanced down the pool to see Sorcha cutting through the water on her breaststroke. The whole family had had a huge discussion about the swimming thing the previous week. Ciara wanted to swim, and swim seriously. She knew she could do well. She was eager to break into the senior cycles and the larger competitions, eventually moving into professional swimming. Mark certainly considered her good enough. But, to really do well, she needed to up her training times.

Sorcha struggled along in her younger sister's wake. She didn't show the same promise at a senior level as Ciara did, even though she was a year older.

But Ciara had to dedicate more time to her training and that meant earlier starts, more hours training and a tougher programme. She nodded her head now in agreement with Mark. He threw his eyes up to heaven. He had more to say about it.

"Nodding is no good, Ciara. Agreeing with me isn't going to improve your times. Look at your pattern. You're on time for fewer than half of your morning sessions."

"I'm always on time for my evening training. You know I come straight from school. I'm always in the pool before you begin. I get here at five and usually get fifteen minutes warm-up done before you begin at twenty past."

"OK, I'll grant you that."

"Big deal," thought Ciara. "Don't get too excited, whatever you do." Mark went on.

13

"But that's only two evenings a week. You really need to up that to four – ideally five – mornings and two evenings of full training time per week. I can then plan your season's training knowing that you're clocking up enough hours to really make a difference."

"I know, I know," Ciara said. "You know I've to get a lift from my dad – so it's not ideal. I think we're going to move house so I can be near the pool and the gym. That won't happen until the spring, but in the meantime, Sorcha and I are changing schools after Christmas. I've just about talked Sorcha round. We're starting at Christian's Secondary, just down the road. We'll be staying in my gran's house until my parents find a new place to live. It means I can get here by five-fifteen or so and can stay on until seven-thirty. And I can do it five mornings a week."

Ciara made it all sound so simple and straightforward. But there'd practically been civil war in the Vaughan household while all this was being decided. Sorcha had hit the roof about changing schools. "What? I'm not going to be with the same friends any more? I've to go to Christian's Secondary? A whole gang of spotty-faced low life to get used to, from every council estate this side of the Liffey. Just so that we can get Ciara to her precious swimming-pool more often? I don't believe this!"

"It's for you too, Sorcha," her mother had explained. "You'll benefit from the extra swimming times."

"Big deal," groaned Sorcha. "I can slog my way up and down the pool an extra twenty times a day now.

14

Whoopee! As well as force my body out of its natural state of sleep two more mornings a week."

"Don't be so smart," their father had intervened. "Even if you don't benefit from the swimming side of things, it'll broaden your experiences. You've never been in a mixed school before. It'll introduce you to new aspects of education – they are renowned for their progressive educational ideas."

"What?" Sorcha couldn't believe the tack the argument was taking. "So now you're going to dump me in a school where self-defence is essential if I want to make it through the day. Don't you know that any inter-schools debate or sports event against Christian's Secondary strikes the fear of God into every other school in the city? I can't believe you're doing this to me. Why can't I stay where I am? I'm happy there. I like it. I'll stay alive!"

Sorcha always made a drama out of anything she was a little put out by. Anyone else might be unhappy. Sorcha would be suicidal. Someone else would be in trouble. Sorcha was about to be murdered. She marched up and down the kitchen now, enjoying the attention.

Until her father had had his fill of it.

"Enough of the melodramatics, Sorcha." He was drawing the argument to a close. "You can't possibly travel halfway across the city every morning to get to your old school. We've discussed this endlessly and this appears an optimum solution all round. It means I'll be closer to work and I won't have to get up at the crack of

15

dawn every morning. Ciara can make her own way to training and can manage it herself. And you can both benefit from the advantages of a new school."

Sorcha had flounced out of the kitchen, tears of rage coursing down her cheeks. She had hardly spoken to Ciara for three days after that discussion. She'd gradually thawed out, but it still wasn't a subject Ciara introduced voluntarily into any conversation with her sister.

When Ciara told Mark, he was brief in his approval. He nodded at her.

"Good. So I can start looking at your training programme and developing it." He glanced at his watch. "Anyway, I don't want your muscles to cool down now. Take some hand paddles and do a six by 50-metre breaststroke, alternating arms and legs on each twenty-five. Then change to legs only and do two by 100 metres. I want to do some work on turns after that. Take lane 3, but make sure you go behind Dónal. He's working on full stroke and you'll only hold him up."

Ciara strapped two plastic paddles on to the palms of her hands and dived in. Mark was never one to show how happy he was, but she guessed he was pleased with her decision. It meant that he'd now be able to look at her training over the season, certain that she'd be here long enough to get it all in. From Ciara's point of view, it meant none of the hassle of relying on her dad to drive her to the pool – which wasn't ideal when there was a gala coming up and she wanted to snatch more time in the pool or to have a talk with Mark about

16

tactics. She'd be her own manager in terms of getting to the pool on time and that was good. She'd now be able to get in five good sessions of two and a quarter hours in the mornings before school. With two sessions of two and a half hours in the evenings and two hours of weights in the gym, she'd be doing almost 18 and a half hours of training per week. That was an increase of four and a half hours on her current work-out times. "Sounds good," she agreed to herself as she eased herself into the rhythm of the stroke and swam towards the shallow end of the pool.

The water resisting against the smooth plastic of the hand paddles made her muscles pull harder, building up her strength so that when she took them off she would skim through the water with greater ease. She was aware of Mark walking alongside her on the bank.

"Don't dip your head too deeply into the water," he shouted at her. "Keep it shallow. Full extension on the legs, Ciara. Concentrate!"

But her mind was thinking now about how she might improve her times in the six months she had before the qualifying heats for the nationals came about. Mark might even put her in for a couple of smaller meets to build up experience, but at the end of the day it was up to her and how much she put into her training.

At seven-ten, the whistle went. Swimmers finished whatever length they were on and climbed out at the deep end of the pool. The coaches moved diving blocks on to the pool edge while Mark called instructions.

"Twenty fifty-metre sprints, individual medley order. All seniors to go first in each team, junior swimmers to the end. On your blocks, first swimmers please."

Ciara was first in her lane. She stepped on to the block, curling her toes round the edge, and stooped low, her knees slightly bent.

"Take your marks, get set . . . go!"

Chapter 2

"Ouch!"

The ruler poked her hard in the back.

"What do you think you're playing at?" hissed Mary-Anne Darke, turning round angrily from her place in the front row to face Edel Lucas, who sat behind her. Edel stared owlishly back through her round spectacles.

Edel's such a swot, thought Mary-Anne irritably, sitting there with her books always open on the right page. Edel's homework was always finished by the right day, in her neat handwriting, laid out in her smooth, flat copybook with paragraphs and margins and headings and red lines. Not like Mary-Anne, who spent her days avoiding handing up her work; when she did, it was usually cogged from somebody else in the class.

And you'd never normally find Mary-Anne sitting in the front row under the teacher's schnozzle. No way. Not like Edel the brainbox, who would sit on the teacher's lap given half a chance. Try the back row for Mary-Anne, swinging on the back two legs of her chair. There was usually some peace back there. Or at least a reasonable distance between you and teacher.

But she never got a bit of peace in Mr Barrett's class.

Old Fat Bat Barrett the science teacher could be guaranteed to haul the most resistant student right to the front row under his watchful eye, like had happened today with Mary-Anne. He got a buzz out of doing that kind of thing. Kind of made you on edge through the whole class, though. Made you jumpy not knowing exactly when he was going to hop on you with some smart question. Not that Edel Lucas minded. She always knew the answers to the questions Mr Barrett asked.

Mary-Anne looked at Edel now, who sat staring at her.

"Don't blame me," Edel replied icily to Mary-Anne's comment. "Blame it on the childish pranks of your immature friends in the back row."

She held out a folded piece of paper, making no attempt to conceal it from the sharp eyes of Mr Barrett. Mary-Anne glanced instinctively up at the teacher, but he was busy finishing his blackboard drawing of the human eye, complete with bloodshot bits and a blue iris. He had drawn it to look as though the unfortunate owner had been stripped of an eyelid, eyelashes and skin. It reminded Mary-Anne of a horror film about a grisly hand that had been chopped off its evil owner. It ran around the place without an arm or a body, like some demented pink crab, throttling its unfortunate victims. Mary-Anne had decided that Mr Barrett's illustration was like a similar film. Perhaps about a scooped-out eyeball from a giant Cyclops that threatened to hypnotise its victims into a deadly trance. She'd even started to draw in an evil-looking eyebrow and wild-looking hair on the version in her copy.

The floating eighteen-inch eyeball on the black-board stared spookily out at the class. Reassured that Fat Bat was happily engaged, Mary-Anne turned her attentions back to the note.

"This apparently urgent communication is from them," Edel continued, clearly bored with the antics of some of her classmates.

Snatching the note, Mary-Anne leaned over in her chair and smirked back at Eoghan and Katie, who grinned and made thumbs-up signals at her through the rows of pupils. Turning round in her seat again, she looked at the note. "URGENT" was written in red pen on one side. Around it, Mary-Anne recognised the swirly bits and dots with which Katie always adorned any heading in her copy. Mary-Anne's name was on the other side. She began opening the note.

"I'll have that please, Miss Darke," announced the voice of Mr Barrett, who appeared suddenly at her side. He leaned right over, speaking into Mary-Anne's ear, and snapped the folded slip from her fingers. She jumped. His sudden appearance startled her, particularly as he had approached silently. The disembodied eyeball was nothing compared to a disembodied teacher. Mary-Anne studied him carefully, checking him out for evil eyebrows and wild woolly hair. Mr Barrett held the note aloft triumphantly, an artificial smile of sympathy plastered over his shiny face. "Unable to cope with separation during the forty minutes of my class, your partners-in-crime deemed it necessary to write to you. How sweet! How endearing!"

"Mr Barrett," cried Mary-Anne. "It's not meant for you. It's got my name on it – look. And I haven't even read it yet."

"Nor shall you, you lowly worm," Mr Barrett answered as he swept back to his chair on the rostrum. The class watched him with amusement. His long black gown billowed out behind him, giving him an uncanny resemblance to a large bat. His undisputed likeness to a mammoth version of that small mammal had earned him his well-deserved nickname. He swished the cloak out behind him as he sat down so it wouldn't get caught beneath his large rear end.

"Continue with drawing the cross-section of the eyeball in full colour," he announced to the rest of the class, "while I entertain myself with the scribblings of fools."

Again, Mary-Anne turned round to catch the eye of Eoghan or Katie, but they were now bent earnestly over their copies, pretending to be totally absorbed in colouring in optic nerves and blood vessels. She sighed. God, that Edel was such an idiot. She couldn't even pass a note discreetly without getting everyone in trouble. Now she, Mary-Anne, would have to wait until break-time to find out what the note was about. She gazed up at Mr Barrett who had finished reading *her* note. He glanced at her over the tops of his glasses.

"Well, Miss Darke, shall I shed a little light on your dreary life?"

She brightened up. Maybe he was going to tell her what was in it after all.

"Yessir," she replied, sitting up expectantly.

"Well then," he continued. "Tonight you can prepare a three-page essay on the effect of light on the organ of the human eye. Perhaps you will then see the importance of paying more attention in class and not getting distracted by utter trivia."

"Come on, Mr Barrett," began Mary-Anne, shrugging sulkily back in her seat again. "How am I supposed to do that?"

Her teacher ignored her and continued speaking.

"And your two allies in the back row can prepare essays on the effect of darkness on the eye and on how the human eye discerns colour."

"What?" cried Eoghan, jerking his head up from his copy, all mock interest in his biology studies abruptly forgotten. "You don't even know I done anything."

"'Did', please! If you must complain, at least use correct grammar to do so," said Mr Barrett.

"Why do we have to do two essays and Mary-Anne has only one to do?" complained Katie.

"You don't have to do two essays," explained Mr Barrett patiently, pressing together the tips of his fingers. Resting his chin on them, he gazed wearily ceilingwards. "Lord, grant me patience," he muttered to himself, then "You have to do one each – one of you shall do an essay on the effect of darkness on the human

23

eye and the other shall do an essay on how the human eye discerns colour. That is the only way I can be sure that you won't all copy each other. And you can fight amongst yourselves as to which essay is assigned to whom."

"I won't do it," announced Eoghan, folding his arms across his chest and rocking back on his chair legs. "My mum will write a note excusing me. You can't make me do nothing I don't want to."

"I'm *not* trying to make you do nothing. You do nothing all the time, and entirely of your own free will," replied Mr Barrett.

"What?" asked Eoghan. He was easily confused.

"For once I am trying to make you do *something*," said Mr Barrett. "If you won't do the essay at home, I can, if I really must, arrange to supervise you after school this evening. But let's not allow it get to that, shall we? I really have far better things to do."

Eoghan looked horrified.

"No way, sir," he answered. "Last time I did that, I didn't get home till after seven. My little brother had eaten my oven chips and my fish-fingers were burnt black. Ended up having bread and jam for my tea, I did."

"Well, then," agreed Mr Barrett amicably. "Why don't you do the essay in the comfort of your own home and save your fish-fingers the torture of being charred? It appears to be far kinder all round. To me most of all."

The bell rang loudly announcing the end of the class.

The room normally exploded into a cacophony of scraping chairs and loud voices once the bell sounded, but not when Mr Barrett was teaching. The students knew better. Mr Barrett waited for a full ten seconds in complete silence, his chin balanced on his fingertips, his eyes gazing reverently at the fluorescent light on the ceiling. On the corridor outside, the sounds of classroom doors being flung open, laughter and voices and masses of feet charging up and down made the silence in the classroom even more obvious. All the while, his class shifted uneasily in their seats, watching him intently. Then, in a voice little louder than a whisper, he said.

"You may now leave, with due respect for both my classroom and my ears. Eoghan, Katie and Mary-Anne, you will please wait behind to speak to me."

The pupils filed out quietly, maintaining a respectable silence until they passed the threshold upon which they broke into the customary yells and charging about.

"This is all your fault," Mary-Anne whispered to Edel as she left the classroom. Edel sniffed at her with disdain and continued out. For one fleeting moment, Mary-Anne was very tempted to grab Edel by the throat there and then and show her exactly how aggrieved she was with the whole event. But, with her teacher standing no more than six feet away, she thought better of it. At that moment, Katie and Eoghan appeared at her side. She turned to them.

"What was in the note, anyway?" Mary-Anne asked. "What was so urgent?"

"It wasn't so much *urgent*, as important," Katie explained.

"What's the difference?" enquired Eoghan, looking at Katie.

"Well," began Katie confidentially, "It's about Miss Keenan. My mum overheard the headmistress talking to her in the staffroom. She's been seeing this fellow for almost a year now . . ."

"Is that it?" asked Mary-Anne, interrupting her. "Is that your news? You mean to tell me you got me a stupid essay about an eyeball just to let me know that one of the teachers has the hots for some guy?"

"No," Katie went on. "That's not it."

"Well, you worthless beings," Mr Barrett began, "if you please."

They stopped their conversation and gathered sullenly around his desk. "Maybe one of you can tell me what battle plans I should prepare next in this continuing war between the three of you and your science work? For the last three months, since coming back to school after the summer, you three have been nothing but trouble in my class. When I sit you together, you snigger and talk and make comments about other people. When I separate you, you insist on sending notes to each other, distracting the other pupils and interrupting my teaching. The only thing worse than your appalling behaviour is your complete failure to submit homework on time and of an acceptable standard."

There was a long silence until Mary-Anne felt the need to fill it.

"Sorry, sir," she muttered, gazing down at the scuffed toes of her shoes.

"Sorry? *Sorry?* Is that it? Mary-Anne, you have failed all but one test this term, and you only managed to scrape a pass in that because you were sitting next to Edel Lucas. You were reasonably able in my class last year – I've never known a worse record of failure."

"I failed *all* my tests this term, sir. I haven't even passed one. That's worse," Eoghan reminded him.

Mr Barrett looked at him dismissively. "Oh, for goodness sake, Eoghan. You've *always* failed my tests, so that doesn't count. At least you're a consistent failure. Mary-Anne used to pass last year." He even looked a bit hurt by it all. "Now, you won't even pass one for me without cheating."

Then he turned to Katie.

"And as for you, young lady. Not only have you got yourself into trouble, but you've demonstrated quite clearly that your mother is not able to keep confidences in relation to her work. It is something that I'm now considering discussing with Mrs Graham. And all because you couldn't wait until breaktime to tell your friend your latest bit of gossip from the headmistress's office."

Katie looked as though she'd been slapped across the face.

"Oh God, Mr Barrett," she began, almost breaking into tears. "I'm really, really sorry. Only don't get my mum into trouble. Please! I know it's all my fault. Eoghan didn't know what I was writing to Mary-Anne. And Mary-Anne never got the note so she doesn't know what's in it. I take all the blame, only don't get my mum

27

into trouble. She'll kill me, she really will. I'll even write the essays for the others tonight."

Mary-Anne looked at Katie in surprise. That kind of offer was most unlike her. Not wishing to miss out, Mary-Anne turned immediately to Mr Barrett.

"I think that's a great idea, sir," she agreed.

Eoghan grinned his approval.

"That's enough, Mary-Anne," Mr Barrett snapped.

Eoghan's face fell – he thought Mary-Anne was on to a winner.

Mr Barrett turned back to Katie.

"I wouldn't like to have your premature death on my conscience, Katie. Not on this occasion, anyway. I may change my mind on that one tomorrow. And I'd like to believe that your mother was a little loose with her tongue just this once. Perhaps, on this occasion, I may overlook it other than advising Mrs Graham to be more discreet when the cleaning staff are in the building." He paused for a second, and then continued with a note of warning in his voice. "But only if I see a noticeable improvement in your work."

Katie looked relieved. "You will, sir. I promise you that. You won't see any more messing from me, you can be sure. I'll have my homework on time from now on. Thanks very much, sir. You won't regret this, I promise."

"Why don't you get down and lick his shoes too?" whispered Mary-Anne to her irately.

"What was that, Mary-Anne?" asked Mr Barrett.

"I was just saying that I think it's great news too," Mary-Anne smiled sweetly.

"I also expect you to pass every test I set between now and Christmas," Mr Barrett continued to Katie.

"Does that mean we get off doing our essays, sir?" enquired Eoghan hopefully.

"Most certainly not," said Mr Barrett. "I expect three essays on my desk at nine in the morning and no excuses. Is that clear?"

"Yessir," they agreed in sulky unison.

"Now get out of my classroom, you amoebic jellies."

At lunch-time, the three of them made their way to the girls cloakroom where they sat on the benches amongst rows and rows of grey uniform coats to eat their lunches. Mary-Anne lit up a cigarette and inhaled deeply.

In the distance, the faint sounds of shouts and the crack of hurls from the sports fields could be heard. Otherwise, the cloakroom was quiet. It was always a peaceful place to have a smoke and a chat. It was out of bounds during lunch-time, in an effort to reduce smokers and general dossers who liked to hang round the empty coats and toilet blocks.

"Fat Bat's a scumbag," muttered Mary-Anne. She began absentmindedly poking the red cigarette tip into the fabric at the cuff of the coat nearest her. "Imagine giving me an essay to do just because I turned around to answer Edel flipping Lucas's poke! *She* should be the one to do this essay, not me. After all, she's the one who passed me the note. I had nothing to do with it. I've a good mind to get her for this."

In her anger, she poked the cigarette harder. A little

shower of sparks glittered momentarily before extinguishing. There was a wisp of smoke as the fabric blackened and burnt.

"Imagine having to do an essay on how darkness affects the human eye. What can I write about?" wondered Eoghan gloomily, watching her actions.

"You could always talk about needing to go to sleep when it's dark," suggested Mary-Anne. She took the cigarette tip out of the little hole she had burnt and began picking at the charred stitching. "After all, that *is* what happens during the night, it gets dark and we all go to sleep."

Eoghan brightened up. "That's it. Darkness has the effect of making the eye go to sleep." He paused and looked puzzled again. "How am I going to fill three pages with that?"

Abandoning her activities with the coat, Mary-Anne held her cigarette tightly between her lips, winced and leaned over a bit. She pulled up the side of her shirt and screwed her head round, trying to peer at her back.

"I bet I've got a great big bruise from Edel's ruler. She tried to crack one of my ribs with it just to attract my attention, did you know that? What a fruitcake! Just let her wait till she needs me to do something for her and watch me drop her straight in it."

"Let me have a look," said Eoghan. He reached over and yanked Mary-Anne's shirt up a bit more. "Ooh. That looks sore."

"Does it?" asked Mary-Anne, genuinely surprised that

he could see anything at all. She twisted her head even more. "I can't see anything."

"Do you want me to rub it better?" asked Eoghan. He stood up eagerly, cracking his knuckles in anticipation.

"Get lost," Mary-Anne told him. She tucked her shirt in again and pushed him off. "You're just looking for an excuse to have a grope." Then, turning to Katie, who had been thoughtfully eating her lunch throughout, she said, "What's the big deal about Miss Keenan, anyway?"

"Yes," said Eoghan, realising that they'd never quite got to the bottom of the whole story. "What's the low-down on her anyway? Did he knock her up?"

Katie gave Eoghan a withering look. "You're gross! You've a one-track mind."

Eoghan shrugged. They waited expectantly.

"Well?" demanded Mary-Anne, when it was clear that Katie wasn't about to reveal any more without being pushed.

"Well what?" Katie opened a bag of salt-and-vinegar crisps and began crunching.

"What's the low-down? Tell us."

Mary-Anne stood right in front of Katie, her hands on her hips. Katie kept eating her crisps, ignoring her. Eoghan sat idly watching Mary-Anne getting annoyed.

"Make her tell us, Eoghan," ordered Mary-Anne.

"What?" asked Eoghan, surprised.

"Go on," Mary-Anne said. "Make her tell us. We want to know, don't we?"

"Yes, we do," agreed Eoghan.

"Then make Katie tell us."

"OK," said Eoghan. He turned towards Katie purposefully. Then he paused and looked back at Mary-Anne. "What'll I do to her?"

"Oh, for crying out loud, Eoghan!" Mary-Anne cried. "Edel isn't the only imbecile around here. Use your imagination, just get the information out of her."

At that moment, a clamour of hurls and footsteps came echoing down the corridor. Katie, Eoghan and Mary-Anne immediately forgot their squabbles and pricked up their ears. The strong voice of Miss Keenan sailed over the clattering and chattering.

"Quick, girls! You'll just have time to change before class begins. That was a great camogie session. Now, if you can repeat that kind of teamwork before the championships, we'll certainly sweep to victory."

Mary-Anne and Katie looked at each other in alarm. Eoghan's face paled at the sound of the teacher's voice.

"Oh, my God," he cried, looking wildly round the girl's cloakroom for somewhere to hide his six-foot frame. "She'll skin me alive if she finds me in here."

While Eoghan legged it to the furthest corner of the cloakroom and tried unsuccessfully to hide himself among the coats, Katie and Mary-Anne waved their hands through the smoke, trying to disperse it in the air. Then they ducked into two toilet cubicles and locked the doors. The camogie players swarmed into the cloakroom, filling the space with a strong odour of fresh air and grass, sweat and energy. They talked and clattered round the place, peeling off their T-shirts and changing their shoes. Sniffing the smoke, Miss Keenan walked boldly into the toilet area and knocked on the doors of the locked cubicles.

"Who's in there?" she demanded. "Come out, please."

"Just a moment," replied Mary-Anne, flushing her butt down the toilet and opening the door. She smiled innocently up at Miss Keenan.

"Hello, Miss," she began. "I'm just on my way to class." She walked over to the washhand basins and turned on the water as Katie opened the door of her cubicle and walked out, also smiling.

Miss Keenan looked at the two of them.

"You know perfectly well that this area is out of bounds during lunch-times. Now, what's going on here?"

The two girls looked at the teacher, but their responses were interrupted by a loud scream from the cloakroom.

"Get out, you pervert!"

Miss Keenan spun round as Eoghan made a clumsy effort to escape through the door. He slithered in an undignified manner on the polished vinyl, before finally getting his footing and disappearing round the corner. Several girls were in hot pursuit, shouting at him in anger.

"Spy on the girls in the changing room, would you?"

"Creep!"

"Peeping Tom!"

"Can't get enough of what you want, eh?"

Even though they were already in trouble, Katie and

33

Mary-Anne couldn't resist sniggering at the sight of the big lout slithering across the changing room floor. Miss Keenan turned back to them, her face now an angry red.

"Right, you two," she told them. "Get down to Mrs Graham's office immediately. And bring that other specimen with you."

Chapter 3

By the time Ciara and Sorcha had showered, dressed in warm track suits and emerged from the steaming warmth of the swimming-pool, it was seven-fifty. Their father's car was parked facing the exit gates, along with the cars of several other parents who had arrived to collect their children. Mr Vaughan sat reading the morning paper, the interior light of the car switched on to illuminate the dull morning.

The day had dragged itself into a bleak and gloomy greyness. There was a dampness in the air that clung to the trees and gathered to shimmering drops on the stark black branches.

Ciara shivered as she opened the back door of the car.

"Why haven't you got your hoods up?" their father enquired as they clambered into the car. "You know you'll catch a chill coming out with wet hair on a cold morning like this."

Ciara immediately pulled her hood up, tying the strings in a loose knot. The closeness of the warm fleece

35

to her skin felt cosy. Sorcha said nothing but just lay back against the headrest, closing her eyes.

"I'm wrecked," she suddenly announced. "The thought of a day at school is killing me."

Her father smiled at her.

"Wait until after your training session this evening," Ciara piped up from the back seat. "You don't know the meaning of the word 'wrecked' until then!"

Sorcha groaned audibly.

Their father started the engine and began the drive back home. The traffic heading into the city had begun to build heavily and, all along Howth Road, cars moved in a continuous stream. Luckily, their homeward journey took them in the opposite direction and they sailed along, passing gathering lanes of traffic.

They arrived into the house to the delicious smell of toast.

"Hi, Mum," Ciara called as she ran upstairs to change into her school uniform. "I'll be down in a minute."

Sorcha arrived up to the bedroom a few moments later, carrying a slice of toast dripping with honey. She bit greedily into the hot toast.

"Mmm! I was famished," she enthused, squeezing past where Ciara was zipping up her school skirt.

"Hey, watch my duvet," Ciara cried as a dribble of honey oozed over the crust and trickled down Sorcha's fingers.

Sorcha scooped it up with one slurp of her tongue. "Never fear! Sorcha the shimmering shadow can catch a drip of honey faster than the speed of sound," she announced. She leaped on to Ciara's bed to get over to her own side of the room. Pausing in the middle, she licked more melting honey from her fingertips and the back of her hand, then stepped back ready to hop across to her own bed. But she was so busy watching the traces of honey slithering from the toast that she completely misjudged her step from one bed to the next. She landed with a crash and a howl between the two beds. The toast went sailing through the air and landed with a sticky splat in the middle of Ciara's pillow. Toasted crumbs scattered around while the honey trickled gleefully down the pillow.

"So much for Sorcha the shimmering shadow – pity she can't learn to look where she's going,' said Ciara; then, as she turned around, she cried indignantly, "Look at my pillowcase!" She leaped over and grabbed the pillow from the bed.

"Never mind me, of course," muttered Sorcha, dragging herself up and on to her bed. "I'm fine, thanks for asking, Ciara. No bones broken this time. No muscles pulled that might affect my training."

There was an anxious call from her mother downstairs. "Are you girls all right?" followed by a less anxious one from their father, "Quit the messing around, you two. Get down for your breakfasts now."

"You idiot. Well, you can have the grotty one, so," Ciara told her as she hauled the honey-sodden pillow-case off her pillow and threw it in the middle of Sorcha's bed. She stripped the pillowcase from her sister's pillow and replaced it on her own, puffing it up and placing it neatly on the bed. Turning to the mirror, she finished tying her tie.

"Where did you put the bit of toast I was eating?" Sorcha enquired.

Ciara looked at Sorcha through her reflection on the mirror.

"It's probably still in the middle of the pillowcase," she replied.

Sorcha rooted around in the crumpled pillowcase and retrieved a battered-looking piece of toast from which she gingerly took a bite.

"Sorcha, you're disgusting," cried Ciara. "Throw it out! It's covered in dust and feathers from the pillow."

Sorcha ignored her and started to change into her school uniform while Ciara finished getting ready and headed downstairs for breakfast. Her mum had already finished and was packing the dishwasher.

"Help yourself, love," she said as her younger daughter walked into the room. "How did training go?"

"Fine."

Ciara poured out a bowl of muesli. She lifted the carton of milk and looked at the label. "Is there any low-fat?"

"I bought some yesterday," replied her mother. "Have a look in the fridge."

"You shouldn't be taking low-fat all the time," her father interrupted. "You girls need calcium and proper nutrients."

Ciara looked at him. "Forget it, Dad. There's as much calcium and stuff in low-fat milk."

"Did you tell Mark about your change of school?" her mum enquired.

"I did."

"And?"

"I think he's pleased. He's never over the moon about anything. He's really concerned about my times for the next season. I'm missing out so much training. Could it not be sooner than Christmas when I change, Mum? It's another five weeks away. That's twenty hours of training I'm missing out on." It only dawned on Ciara as she spoke just how much training she was missing in such a short time. "Oh, my God. Twenty hours! That's, like, enough time to work on an entire pre-season programme in one stroke. Can't you ring the principal or something? Tell her I really need to get started."

"Ciara," her father said looking up from buttering his toast, "calm down and eat your breakfast or you'll be late for school. We've been through all of this before. It's out of the question that you change sooner than that. Christian's Secondary would prefer you to begin in a new term. Your present school want you to sit the Christmas exams so they can send on a final report. And there's no way you can expect Gran to have you two to stay with her in the run-up to Christmas."

Ciara sat down heavily with her muesli and two Pop Tarts. Sorcha trotted into the kitchen and helped herself to cereal and fruit.

"Look at the time!" Mrs Vaughan suddenly exclaimed. "I wanted to be early this morning. Now I'm going to be late. I wish you wouldn't keep me talking." With that, she scooted out of the kitchen to finish getting ready for work.

There was silence for a while, then Mr Vaughan spoke again.

"Sorcha, are you interested in upping your training to five mornings between now and Christmas? A short, sharp burst to drop your personal best times by a couple of seconds?"

Sorcha pulled a face, while Ciara jerked her head up suddenly, not quite believing what she heard her father say. Was he suggesting driving them to the pool two extra mornings a week? Sorcha finished her mouthful of cereal so slowly that Ciara thought she was going to hit her.

"I don't think my personal bests are going to improve with a short, sharp burst of anything other than anabolic steroids," commented Sorcha. "So, thanks for the offer, but I think I'll stick to the bed."

Her father nodded and returned to eating. Ciara stared at him.

"Dad!"

He glanced up enquiringly.

"What about *my* personal bests? Aren't you going to give me the option of dropping mine too?"

"Yours?" Her father frowned. "Your personal bests. Are you serious?"

Ciara was confused. "What do you mean am I serious? Have you gone nuts?"

Her father smiled slightly. "My dear Ciara, I didn't

even think it was something I'd have to ask you about. I automatically assume that you'll be waiting at the front door for me every weekday morning at five-thirty from now on. Am I right?"

Ciara grinned, her father's meaning suddenly clear.

"You mean," she started in disbelief, a big grin spreading across her face, "you're going to bring me to the pool *every* day between now and Christmas? Are you really? You'll bring me for an extra two days until I change schools?"

Mr Vaughan broke into a broad smile while Ciara gave a whoop of delight and leaped off her seat to hug him.

"I can't believe it," she said. "An extra four hours a week, starting next week!"

"Let's break open the champagne," Sorcha muttered dryly into her cereal bowl.

"You can start tomorrow, if you really want. Only you have to take the responsibility of getting both of us up and out in time. I've done it for long enough, so now you can take the alarm-clock and set it each evening. It'll prove how dedicated you really are."

"Dad, you're brilliant!" Ciara said.

"Well, just make sure that alarm-clock is kept under your pillow so I'm not disturbed more than necessary," Sorcha warned.

It was twenty to nine when the two sisters left their home to walk the fifteen minutes to school. Ciara was halfway through third year, Sorcha was in transition year, having finished her Junior Cert.

"It's such a bummer having to change schools," Sorcha began. "I mean, don't you hate all the fuss and upheaval?"

Ciara had to be careful how she answered this one. Sorcha was still smarting from having to change schools. She was not impressed with having to do it mainly for her sister's sake.

"To be perfectly honest, I can't wait," Ciara replied earnestly. "Take, for example, my 400-metre Individual Medley. At the moment, it's at 5 minutes 7 seconds. The qualifying time for the 400-metre IM at the Leinster Pools Meet is 5.01. The entries have to be sent in eight weeks time. So that means I have to knock *six* seconds off my time between now and then. If Dad hadn't offered to bring me to the two extra sessions, that would have only given me roughly twelve hours a week to bring my time down. There's no way I could manage it. And that's only one event. I was hoping to swim in the 200-metre IM, the 200-metre freestyle and the 200-metre 'fly. But the same story follows with all my strokes."

Sorcha looked sideways at her younger sister as they walked along. Ciara was always doing this kind of thing. You asked her a question, any old question; it could be about the colour of the sky or how many Chinamen it took to build the Great Wall, and she'd manage to answer it by explaining about her swimming and how her training was going. It didn't matter what the question was really about, Ciara didn't mind, it was always about swimming in the end, anyway. Ciara could turn any question right round, no matter how complicated, and suddenly, hey-presto, she had a question about swimming to answer. She could chat away for hours about that.

Sorcha went on impatiently. "For once, I don't mean your swimming, Ciara. I mean, Christian's Secondary is a mixed comprehensive run by a bunch of headcases. Half of them are wired to the moon, and the other half are short of a few marbles. And that's just the teachers! So you can imagine what the kids are like. Won't it kill you not being with the same friends any more? That's what's cracking me up. We've been with the same group of people since, well, pretty much infant school. That's a long time, Ciara. More than eleven years for me, and ten for you."

Ciara thought for a moment. To be perfectly honest, the people she was in school with didn't feature as part of the equation. OK, sure, they were a good group of people. She got on well with them and there was a crowd of them that went round together during breaks. But, no, she had to admit that they just weren't top of her list of priorities. Any free time she had, Ciara's head was full of her swimming. She thought about her turns and how to perfect them. She ran through race tactics in distance swims. She juggled around ideas about training.

But Ciara knew Sorcha was different.

Sorcha only just hung in with the heavy swimming

schedule and, even then, she wavered a bit when the weather was bleak or if she'd had a late night. Admittedly, she nearly always made it to training. She trained hard when she was there. And she always swam in the meets and galas. She did well, too. Clocked up good times and would be a great sprinter if she really worked at it. She was a better build for sprinting than for distance swimming.

But she wouldn't die for her swimming.

She wouldn't put it in front of everything else.

She wouldn't give up her whole life just for her swimming.

Ciara didn't know if she herself would be a champion swimmer, but she was definitely going to try. And if it took a change in home and school and anything else that needed changing, she was prepared to do it.

"It doesn't worry me too much," she replied honestly. "I'm not in with a gang like you are. I mean, you go out for coffee and ice cream and stuff with the girls after school. And you meet up with people on Saturdays, you walk round town with your mates. That's not really me, Sorcha."

"I know that," Sorcha acknowledged. "You spend your time upstairs in the bedroom doing stomach crunches. Or ploughing up and down a pool. Or jogging round in circles till you drop. You'll probably fit in like a dream with the fruitcakes in Christian's. All you can talk about is swimming and racing and times and galas. But that's all too narrow, Ciara. You're so obsessed with swimming that nothing else features. You're only fourteen. You need to get a life."

Ciara burst out laughing at her sister's concern. But Sorcha wasn't laughing. She was serious. Ciara straightened her face and cleared her throat.

"Sorry, Sorcha," she muttered in deference to her sister's expression. "But you don't have to worry. I have a life. And I love it. What more do I need to talk about but swimming? It *is* my life."

"I don't think it's healthy for you, that's all. You're my kid sister. I worry about you messing your life around with all this swimming lark. And I worry more about you messing *my* life around for this swimming lark, too!"

"If you think it's such a 'lark', why do you haul yourself out of the bed three mornings a week?" Ciara asked her. "Why do you get out of the house come rain or shine to train three evenings a week? You sure don't do it for fun, so you must be getting something pretty significant out of it too."

Sorcha nodded.

"Of course I get something out of it. I love swimming, too. I like the buzz of a gala. I feel good when I beat my personal best. And even better when I beat someone else. Sure – all of that's great. I'm just saying that it's not all there is to life. You have to chill out a bit. Let your hair down. Catch the beat, you know; get into other interests."

She looked at Ciara as they walked in the gate of

their school. "And I'm certainly not impressed with hauling up every root I ever laid down and running halfway across the city to start attending Crackpot Academy for the sake of a swimming-pool."

Without a further word, she turned abruptly from Ciara and made her way to her first class.

Chapter 4

"Eoghan!"

Eoghan didn't answer. Why bother? he thought. Any second now and his mother would call again, anyway. She always shouted for him twice. It was a habit of hers and Eoghan wasn't about to break with tradition. He knew she didn't really expect him to respond to her first call.

True enough, there was a pause for a moment or two and then the voice called again.

"Eoghan!"

It was a tone or two higher, usually a sign that she was getting a little impatient. Eoghan stretched across to the door from where he lay on his bed. With his foot, he pushed it closed. He needed some peace for himself without being yelled at by his mother. His room was empty for once, the two brothers who shared with him off playing hurley or football. Their schoolbags were flung across the empty beds.

Eoghan needed to sort his head out and work through some of the bother he was in.

Turning over to his stereo, he hit the "up" volume and the music blared out even louder. It helped him to think when his brains were being blasted out at the same time. It numbed his thoughts.

And, anyway, this was the best bit. He didn't want to miss it.

It was a great dance album he was playing and the number that was now on was amazing. It really thumped in your chest. Especially if you turned the volume up real loud. Eoghan lay back on the bed and let the rhythms wash over him. He could feel his ears zinging.

But not for long.

A second later, the bedroom door burst open and his mother marched in. She didn't even knock or call out to let Eoghan know of her arrival. This was the kind of invasion of his personal space that really bugged him. You'd think being in your own room, with the door closed and grooving away to some great music, people would have some respect for your need for privacy.

But no, not Eoghan's mother. She didn't know the meaning of the word.

"Did you hear me calling you?" she demanded of her son. "God, you can't hear yourself think with that racket."

She reached down and switched off the CD, just like that, cutting off the cool beat and leaving Eoghan's ears throbbing with hunger for it.

"Mam!" bellowed Eoghan, sitting bolt upright on

the bed with fury. "What the hell do you think you're doing? First you march in here like a sergeant-major and then you start interfering with my stuff. I could have been standing here totally naked. This is *our* room and it's out of bounds to anyone unless they have permission."

That kind of outburst never endeared Eoghan to his mother. A more serious, mature approach might hold some water, but he'd blown all opportunity for that this time round. His mother put her hands on her hips and looked at him with a beady eye.

"Don't you give me that cheek, lad. You're not beyond a good box on the ears and, mark my words, you'll get it. Of course you're not going to be standing here naked. Why on earth would you be standing stark naked in the middle of your room at six o'clock in the evening?"

Eoghan made some incoherent splutters of rebellion, but knew not to step beyond the mark. There was no point. He could easily find himself grounded for a week, and that would be Saturday night on the town out the window. His mother went on.

"If you answered me when I called you, there'd be no need for me to come near this pigsty. You certainly don't think I come here by choice, do you? You'd never know what you'd pick up here." She looked distastefully round the room. "Come down to the kitchen. I need the potatoes scrubbed."

"I'm not having dinner here tonight." Eoghan replied. He slid a shade of impudence into his voice, but not enough to make it sound too brazen. It rolled off his mother like water off a duck's back.

"Don't be trying to worm your way out of it. The potatoes still need to be scrubbed, whether you're eating here or not. Downstairs to the kitchen, please. Now!"

God, this kind of supervision as if he were a kid was too much. Eoghan stomped noisily downstairs and took the basin from the sink.

"How many do you want?" he asked as he clattered noisily into the utility room where the vegetables were kept.

"About eighteen. Make sure they're of even size," his mother instructed him.

A few moments later, Eoghan stood at the kitchen sink, scrubbing the earth off the skins of the potatoes. His two youngest brothers struggled over their homework at the kitchen table behind him. His mother was covering a heap of fish fillets with egg and breadcrumbs. And the radio droned on about a forthcoming general election and the policies of the opposing parties. Eoghan was in a foul mood.

Life was a drag.

Miss Keenan had frogmarched them up to the headmistress's office straight after lunch. That had caused Eoghan major grief. He'd been accused of spying on the girls changing in the cloakrooms. At least Katie and Mary-Anne had been caught too, and they could hardly be accused of the same thing. And Mary-Anne had been smoking whereas he hadn't, so that let him off the hook somewhat. Anyway, Eoghan couldn't have concealed himself in the coats even if he'd wanted to. His longs legs and arms stuck out all over the place, which is why he was seen straight off. Mrs Graham couldn't genuinely believe he was attempting to peek. He'd have to be really stupid to expect to get away with hiding like that.

They'd told Mrs Graham that they'd been hanging round the cloakrooms all that lunch-time, just chatting and dossing, but she wasn't convinced; mainly because Mary-Anne and Katie had been caught smoking on more than one occasion before. And Eoghan had been stupid enough to get caught misbehaving with a first-year girl the previous term. They'd been larking around in the bushes at the back of the boiler-house, having mitched out of class. It had all been a bit of a joke, nothing too serious. Just a bit of necking. Anyway, the caretaker had come across the two of them when he was out having a smoke and had reported it to the year-heads of both years. They'd both been put on probation for the rest of the term and given a severe warning. Eoghan had got a heavy dressing-down at the time about his behaviour and responsibilities as a young man. Worse again, his father had been informed. Eoghan had been given a right grilling at home and told to keep his nose clean in future.

And now, here was Mrs Graham with some new evidence to chalk up against him – Peeping Tom! Great, his father would be thrilled about that one.

What talk did that trigger off in Mrs Graham's juke-box of lectures?

Eoghan had stared moodily at the floor while Mrs Graham had spluttered her shock and disappointment.

"Eoghan, for goodness sake. Try to leave some potato behind to cook."

His mother's voice cut in on his daydreaming. Blinking, he looked down at the potato in his hand which now resembled a small, bleached Brussels sprout.

"Sorry," he muttered, putting it back into the water and taking up the next one.

Later on, back in his bedroom, Eoghan turned on his CD again, raised the volume and shut the door. When his brain was well and truly soft-boiled from the music, he considered his fate.

Two-week suspension.

That had been the threat.

And it was no idle one.

If he had one more black mark on his behaviour card between now and the end of the year (good grief, the end of the year, a whole six months away!), the school would suspend him for two full weeks. Only one black mark. He wasn't even going to be given a second chance before suspension would be dished out to him. He knew he stood little chance of getting away with it. You got a black mark for doing *nothing* in his school, he thought dismally.

Ray, his pal in technical drawing, had been given a black mark for writing his girlfriend's name on the wall of the jacks. Everyone did that – it was just what you did. It was what the wall of the toilet block was for. But his school had to hand out black marks for it.

Eoghan himself had been given a black mark last week for not handing in his Irish homework on time. What kind of an education was he getting if Irish homework was considered important enough to get black marks over? Why, he asked himself, did he have to write about the lifestyle of some old woman who lived on a heap of rocks in the Atlantic Ocean about fifty years before he was born? He tried asking them that. But would they listen?

You must be joking.

"Do what you're told or get a black mark," they said to him. He argued with that, but got a black mark for being cheeky. He lost the rag a bit then and told them to stuff their black marks where the sun never shines. He got given a double black mark for that one. Three black marks in a week equalled detention on Friday. Mr O'Donnell, the frog-faced, four-foot little pipsqueak of an Irish teacher who was dishing out his black marks with inordinate glee looked up at him crossly.

"Eoghan, we can keep going like this until you have no detention days left this term. But it's a rather foolish exercise that won't achieve very much. Now you can complain all you want, but having an understanding of Irish culture helps you to have a broader understanding of other nationalities. If you don't want to hand in the homework, I'll give you another double black mark and be done with it. If, however, you agree to do the work during Friday's detention period, you can hand it up to me on Monday morning and no more will be said. Now which is it to be?"

It was a sneaky way of putting no option into a multi-choice question. Mr O'Donnell made it look like he was giving him a choice, but Eoghan knew he was caught good and proper. He had no choice at all at the end of the day – it was a matter of choosing the lesser of two evils.

And he had to stick to his principles.

A double black mark it was, so.

It was the same now with his suspension threat. There were no options there either. Whatever way he looked at it, the future was bleak. If he argued with the punishment, he'd get a black mark, which meant immediate suspension. He knew he wouldn't survive the rest of the year on good behaviour. If he got one measly black mark, all he had to do was sneeze during class and that would be it, he was out of school for two weeks.

His old man wouldn't tolerate that.

Eoghan knew he'd get a good hiding for messing around with his education. He shuddered to think of his father's reaction if he was suspended for two weeks from school.

"Do you think Fat Bat will report us as well?" Mary-Anne had asked as they'd left the office half an hour later.

"No," replied Katie. "I don't think he's quite so corrupt."

Eoghan looked at them glumly. "It won't make much difference to me," he said. "There's not much more punishment she can dish out to me at this stage."

But they were both wrong.

Fat Bat *did* report the essay assignments he'd given them to Mrs Graham, along with telling her about the grief they'd all given in his class since the beginning of term. That was a real sly move of his and won him no favours. There was no real need to report the essays. Whatever about Eoghan and Mary-Anne, poor old Katie had been beside herself with panic when their names had been called out over the intercom to go up to the Head's office. "Oh, my God!" she'd cried. "That's me gone for my tea."

As it happened, Fat Bat hadn't mentioned the contents of the note.

Mrs Graham was determined to believe the worst of them – the day that was in it and all. She'd given them a second earful about poor attitude and lack of effort. She'd gone on and on about bleak futures and no jobs. She'd nearly sent Eoghan to sleep with her lecture on immaturity and the state of the country's young.

He'd heard most of it so many times before that he could easily have stood up there and then and given the whole roasting himself. The thought had crossed his mind as he sat in front of the principal and Fat Bat. He'd given a little chuckle at the idea of it, in spite of himself. He could just see the two of them wearing school uniforms, with fat, dimpled knees and school caps on, sitting morosely in front of him while he read them the riot act from behind the desk. Unfortunately, he'd chuckled just as Mrs Graham was asking them what they had to say for themselves. Mary-Anne and Katie had muttered some pathetic little bit about being sorry and trying better in future. For them, it had even sounded convincing. Mrs Graham then turned to Eoghan, and there he was, sitting with a big, broad grin plastered on his face.

That really put the cat among the pigeons.

Mrs Graham could be a decent enough skin if you knew how to look appropriately remorseful and grovelled a bit. But if you looked cheeky or had a devil-may-care expression, she'd hit the roof.

And that's what she did then.

That kind of outrageous impudence and downright brazenness was not going to be tolerated in *her* school. No more games on Wednesday afternoons for Eoghan until Easter, it was study time every week from now on (he usually mitched off games anyway). He also had detention for the next two weeks. On top of that, they had the essays given to them by Fat Bat.

They were dismissed in disgrace.

"What were you hoping to achieve by laughing like a demented hyena in there?" Mary-Anne demanded as soon as they were out of earshot. "You might have guessed that Graham would go berserk. What were you playing at?"

"I don't know," Eoghan replied. "I just got bored and was thinking of something else. A grin just happened to be on my face when she looked at me."

"'Just happened to be on your face?' And who exactly do you think put it there, you plonker? It was hardly your fairy godmother tripping around with her wand, was it?" Katie responded. "You could have got us all in more trouble, you big lug."

"Eoghan!"

There was his mother again from downstairs. God, was he going to get no peace?

"Eoghan!"

This time, he leaped off the bed and tore the door of the room open.

"What is it?" he roared down at her impatiently.

"Mary-Anne's on the phone for you."

"Oh." Eoghan hadn't even heard the phone ring. "OK. I'm coming down now."

He ran in and turned off the music before going downstairs and picking up the phone in the hall.

"Hi."

"Hi, Eoghan. Are we still meeting in the snooker hall for chips?"

"Sure. What time?"

"Round eight. Katie's coming too."

"OK. See you at eight, so."

Eoghan put the phone down and went into the kitchen.

"I'm heading out in a while," he announced.

"Only if you've finished your homework," his mother replied, flipping the fillets on the pan.

"And you've to be home here by ten sharp," his father added, walking into the kitchen from the utility room. He glanced at his dad in annoyance.

His parents were always doing that kind of thing. Each of them had these little rules that they tagged on to whatever the other said. The two of them were like a double act – Laurel and Hardy or Beavis and Butthead didn't hold a torch to them. Only his mum and dad's was a double parenting act: shared rule-making. Eoghan's father had a different rule that went with each comment Eoghan's mother made. And vice versa. Whoever set the first rule, the other tweaked it a little tighter, just to drive it home. His mother might say "Turn the music down a bit," and his father would add "or I'll confiscate your stereo."

Or maybe he'd say "Eoghan, put the bins out," and his mother would pipe up "and polish the shoes while you're at it." What? Polish the shoes while you're at it. What did putting the bins out have to do with polishing shoes? They were hardly the same kind of job, were they?

Eoghan hated their little habit. It was like some kind of game they played after their sons had gone to bed in the evening. He could just imagine his parents cooking up their little table tennis schemes: "OK, you say this, and then I'll add that." Or "how about I say this *after* you've told them that?"

What a buzz.

"Ten o'clock? Come on, Dad, give me till half past at least. We'll hardly have any time otherwise."

"Good grief, you see the Mob all day every day at school. What more do you need to talk about? OK, ten-fifteen then, and that's final.'

Eoghan was just about to leave the kitchen when his mother added, "But don't forget to do your homework first."

Chapter 5

It was immediately after Christmas when Ciara and Sorcha moved in with Granny.

"I didn't know girls needed so much stuff," their father grumbled as he delivered the third carload of boxes and cases to their granny's house, which was close to the school and, more importantly, to the swimming-pool. "What have you packed in these things – rocks?" he said as he struggled upstairs.

Ciara smiled guiltily as she stood on the front door-step with Gran, who was beaming.

"Now, son," said Granny. "All girls need lots of bits and pieces when they're away from home. You leave my two fine granddaughters alone and don't be asking them personal questions."

"It made sense to bring almost everything as we won't be back in the old house again," Sorcha told her father as she carted armfuls of clothes upstairs.

It took most of the Saturday to move them in. Granny had a big house that she lived in all alone and she was delighted to have the girls' company until their parents found a new place to live. She'd given them a room each, full of old mahogany furniture with hand-stitched eiderdowns on the beds.

"Now, you girls come and go when you like," Granny told them. "I've left alarm-clocks in your rooms and you know your own routines, so just work away and don't mind me."

"Thanks, Gran." Ciara kissed her.

"We'll be around every evening to help prepare a dinner and see the girls," their mum told Gran. "And we'll do the weekly shopping."

"There's no need for that," Granny told her. "I'll pop a few extra items on the shopping list. They're only two wee slips of girls."

"Don't be fooled by appearances," said their dad. "They'll eat you out of house and home, so be prepared."

The following week, they started in Christian's Secondary. Ciara was put into a third-year class. It felt a bit weird at first. For a start, it was odd seeing boys' faces mixed among the girls. And the different uniform took a bit of getting used to. She was accustomed to dark green and cream, now everyone was kitted out in navy and grey.

Not to mention the teachers.

In her old school, the teachers all wore smart suits and sharp little heels that clipped round the wooden floors. Here, the teachers seemed to get away with anything; track suits and jeans, T-shirts and open-neck shirts. Over their clothes, some of them wore black

61

gowns that looked even more out of place, especially if they had denim shirts underneath.

And the kids talked to the teachers like they were talking to their own friends in the school-yard or their parents at home. They were full of "For crying out loud, sir," and "You never told us that, miss;" stuff that Ciara would never have dreamed of saying to her teachers. And if she had, the teachers in her old school would have just curled up and died of fright on the spot because nobody spoke to them out of turn. It just wasn't the done thing. In her old school, you sat in your seat and quietly put up your hand if you wanted to ask something. Or you grouched about the homework or the class-work to your friends if you needed to. But you never, ever complained to the teachers about work being pointless or boring.

Here, it worked both ways. There was none of this "I'm the teacher and you're the pupil, so back in your box and have some respect" kind of attitude. It was more like everyone was in an all-out struggle to get through school and out the other end in one piece. It was basic survival of the fittest – teachers and students all in it together.

The teachers would talk to students like they were their equals, not their inferiors. It was quite usual to hear a teacher challenging someone with "Oh, sure! How do you know that's going to cancel out the equation? Come up here to the blackboard and prove it, then," or "Why would I bother doing that? What difference is a debate going to make to your French?"

That kind of stuff seemed to go on all the time in Christian's Secondary. It was fine to moan about the work. Or even to have a regular conversation with your mate in the middle of class.

In one of Ciara's new classes, the students were writing down a heap of maths exercises from the board. They were all reasonably quiet, except for the usual background rumbling of pencils being sharpened, people muttering to themselves, sniffing, pages being torn out and crumpled up. Next thing, this guy in front of Ciara turned right round in his seat.

"You going down to the soccer match this afternoon, Necker?" he asked his friend, who was sitting in the back row. But he didn't lower his voice or anything. He just spoke right out loud as though there wasn't a class going on at all but just a regular old chat in the school-yard.

Ciara couldn't believe it.

Nobody else seemed even to register it, except Necker who replied out loud to his pal about how his team had done in some match the previous week. All the other students just kept working right on, mumbling and scribbling.

And, what's more, the teacher didn't bat an eyelid. Ciara seemed to be the only one who was fazed by it. The teacher just lifted her head from correcting copies and said calmly, "Oliver, have you finished the work yet? Come on. Less chatter." As if it was the most natural thing in the world for someone to start having a conversation about football right in the middle of a maths class.

63

Otherwise, the lessons were more or less like her last school. Christian's Secondary had smaller classes and more classes in each year.

Fitting in her training every morning was just a dream – there was virtually no effort involved in getting there early and managing a full session. And it was so close that it wasn't like travelling at all. Ciara still couldn't believe how much of a difference it was making to her already.

Sleeping in a strange bed in Granny's house, with the window in another part of the wall and no Sorcha to listen to snuffling around during the night, Ciara woke at four-forty for the first week or so, well before her alarm went off. Sometimes, the rain was sleeting against the window in rattling sheets and it was still dark, making it very tempting to stay in bed. But granny had the heating on early in Ciara's room and it was nice and toasty when she hopped out of bed.

The first morning, Ciara scuttled into Sorcha's room and shook her sister by the shoulder.

"Sorcha," Ciara whispered, not wanting to wake her gran. "Sorcha. I'm going to the pool. Are you coming?"

"You go on," Sorcha mumbled through gummy lips. She turned over in the bed and was sound asleep again by the time Ciara closed the door softly on her way out.

Ciara returned to her room and pulled on her track suit. She was ready to leave for swimming by four-fifty. Because she was cycling, she pulled on waterproofs over her track suit.

The cycle to the pool was wet and muddy and cold, but Ciara was there in ten minutes flat. Even Martha in her little office was surprised to see her so early.

"You're getting awful eager in your old age," she exclaimed as Ciara wheeled her bike into the reception area of the pool. "I don't even have all the lights on in the pool yet."

"Can I leave this here, Martha?" Ciara asked, propping her bike against the wall.

"Not blocking the reception area you can't, but if you want to bring it through my office to the cleaning store, it'll be safe there."

"Thanks," Ciara said as she wheeled her bike through.

When she came through from the changing rooms, Ciara saw what Martha meant. The pool had lights on only at the office end. The rest was in darkness, an inky sheet of shimmering water. The floats from the ropes dividing the lanes drifted lazily in the water's oily movement. Ciara's footsteps in her pool shoes sounded hollow and echoing in the emptiness as she made her way to the middle lane, at the deep end. She looked over the edge to where the deep water seemed to stretch to infinity, the floor of the pool lost in the darkness of the water.

Ciara felt her stomach doing a little flip from the thrill of being the first in the pool. The first to break the calm stillness of the smooth water. The first to shatter the polished surface into a million pieces of liquid crystal.

She stood on the pool edge and curled her toes over the tiles. Bending over, she tensed her muscles, paused for a moment to savour the power, and launched herself in the air, arching into a streamlined arrow that pierced the cool water and plunged her into a smothered silence, so sweet, so complete.

Ciara completed a 400-metre freestyle warm-up with ease, her muscles warming into a strong rhythm, her stretching hands cutting the water smoothly. She considered each stroke, positioning her hand well, concentrating on a regular kick, allowing her body to rotate naturally towards the pull of each arm. Her breathing was relaxed and measured, alternating from side to side. She counted her strokes from pool-end to pool-end as Mark had told her, pacing herself and getting to learn her own stroke-length and count.

By the time she stopped for a twenty-second break, she noticed the pool lights were on full, flooding the interior with a brilliance that made the water shine brightly.

Ciara preferred the darkness. It was somehow easier to focus in the dimness. It helped her to think of her stroke, not to be distracted by flickering shadows and diamonds of brightness reflected on the floor of the pool. The artificial lighting now appeared harsh and cold, glaring off the white tiles, making the disturbed water flash discordantly.

Ciara launched into an easy breaststroke, working on her rhythm, ignoring speed. She was halfway through 200 metres when Mark walked through the small pool room where floats and paddles and ropes were kept and on to the poolside. He sorted out his clipboard and papers and began chalking up the day's programme on the blackboard. Then he walked to the top of the pool, watching Ciara's stroke as he did so.

He allowed her to finish her distance without interruption. She stopped at the end of the 200, pulling herself up out of the water and on to the poolside.

"Hi, Mark. I've finished my warm-up," she told him.

He nodded, smiling slightly. "At five-twenty? That must be a record."

Ciara grinned. Mark continued, pulling a sheet from the back of the bundle on his clipboard.

"I've done up an entire season's programme for you, based on 20 weeks. It's structured around the meets this season, finishing with the national championships in June."

He scanned the sheet on which he'd written Ciara's training programme. He looked up, studying her face as he continued. "Now, Ciara, I'm telling you straight that it's a tough programme. It won't be easy. But you'll be well able for it if you persevere, and you'll be a terrific swimmer at the end. It's geared specially for you, focusing on your strengths during the build-up before meets, and working up your technique and skills during slack periods between galas. I've included dry-land training to spot-build muscles."

"Am I swimming in many galas between now and the national championships?"

"Only two. The Silver Fish meet in Manchester and the Leinsters here. The Silver Fish will be more of a training meet shortly before the nationals, a chance to test your stamina a few weeks before the real thing. As you know, it's swum in a fifty-metre pool, which in itself will be good experience for you. We'll see if it impacts on your times. The Leinsters is a preliminary gala in advance of the national championships. The Leinsters is in May."

Ciara nodded her approval, trying to appear calm, but feeling excitement well up inside her like tiny fireworks that fizzled and crackled.

"OK," said Mark. "Less talking. Let's get down to training."

It was usually about twenty minutes later when Sorcha struggled her way into the changing room and peeled off her track suit. She yawned. This early morning swimming lark was no great shakes when you had to get yourself out of bed. Having Ciara to haul you out of the bed and a car waiting outside to give you a lift to the pool was one thing, but having to get up yourself and then cycle through the rain at five in the morning was no joke.

Almost every time she paddled through the foot-bath and emerged into the pool area, Mark would be there to meet her. True to form, he tapped the face of his watch enquiringly.

"I thought you might have been down here with your

sister," he'd commented. "You've missed half the warm-up, Sorcha. Not looking good for the season."

Sorcha couldn't even be bothered replying. She was still stupid with sleep and it was all she could do to focus her eyes on the swim programme on the blackboard.

Mind you, she thought to herself as she plunged into the water and began her warm-up, whatever about this swimming carry-on, Christian's Secondary was turning out to have more appeal than she thought. Pretty OK school, in her book. Sure, she'd only had a few days there so far but, even so, it was bearable. In fact, it was even enjoyable, she admitted to herself. But she'd rather die than admit that to anyone right now. This was supposed to be a major upheaval for her and she wasn't about to cast aside the sympathy votes she was getting because of that. So she'd struggle on courageously for a bit longer, milk the sympathy from her parents and let them ease up a bit on her training schedules.

Once you were actually in the school, the wild behaviour of the pupils that gave the place a fearsome reputation wasn't such a big deal any more. The reputation the school had was born of fear of the unknown, Sorcha decided. Although the place was full of loudmouths and smart alecks, they seemed to be OK once you weren't the target of their remarks.

In fact, some of them were quite funny.

And there were no holds barred on the stuff they might come out with, even in front of the teachers. Sorcha wasn't used to hearing such open talk about literally *everything* before, particularly when there were boys around, not to mention teachers.

But that wasn't an issue in Christian's.

It was mainly the boys who kept making wisecracks and breaking their hearts laughing at stupid things. They'd really go over the top with their reactions in class, like falling off their chairs or horsing around the place. Sorcha got a buzz from listening to them and watching their antics.

And it wasn't just in classes that they were amusing. They were general all-round entertainment, like an in-school comedy club. They were so easy to read that Sorcha felt she'd got the measure of them from the word go. There was nothing concealed, what you saw was what you got. If they liked you, fine, you were included in their jokes or ignored completely or maybe even spoken to with a bit of sincerity. If they didn't like you, there was no mercy and you were the butt of every rotten joke and insult they could throw at you. That was the case with one girl in Sorcha's class – an unfortunate called Edel who was a real eager beaver from the first time you met her. She even looked a total bookworm with her specs slipping down her nose and her intense expression. The guys had no time for Edel, and, boy, did they give her a hard time.

It was a good lesson to learn from the first day. Sorcha certainly knew not to brandish her books too much or go around looking like a real study-geek.

The girls in her class were harder to get to know and Sorcha hadn't decided about them yet. They hung round in groups with loads of eye make-up caked on them, looking like a pack of ghouls that had escaped from a graveyard. Every corner of the school seemed to be the haunt of a group of transition year students. But it seemed to be only the transition years that behaved like that; no other pupils loitered with intent on school corridors.

And none of the teachers interfered.

Maybe it was the year that was in it, Sorcha concludeed.

In her old school, transition year was spent rushing round trying a heap of work experiences to decide if you wanted to become a physiotherapist or a tropical flower horticulturist or a Superquinn bag packer. You hardly ever saw the transition years as they were always off somewhere helping blind people cross the road or interviewing old people for projects on social justice.

But not in Christian's Secondary.

Here, the transition year girls used it to establish their street cred. The school corridors were their nurseries before progressing on to real street corners. It was hard to get a handle on these ultra-cool streetwise babes.

Sorcha wasn't quite tuned in and found it hard to switch to their wavelength. While the guys were up front, the girls were shady. In their projects, instead of doing work on the Irish taxation system or the local history of the area, they were working on projects about body-piercing, and tattoos.

That was most of them, anyway. Then there were the few hangers-on who fretted around the edges of the main bunch, like rejected wolf cubs in the wild, never quite making it.

Oddballs like Edel.

But Sorcha didn't plan to be like Edel. She'd stick with the lads for the moment, until she found her feet and sorted out which of the girls to hang out with.

Chapter 6

Eoghan watched the new girl, Sorcha Vaughan, as she made her way through the rows of tables to the only seat left in the class. Right at the front, under Fat Bat's nose. What a place to sit in for the first of old Fat Bat's lessons, he thought.

Some baptism of fire.

Eoghan would have hated that.

"Look where that new girl has to sit," he whispered to Mary-Anne. "Wouldn't like to be her."

Mary-Anne looked up and grinned. "Fat Bat can climb all over her and give her a real grilling," she said. "Why don't you offer to swop places if you're feeling sorry for her?"

"No way," replied Eoghan. "With Fat Bat ready to do a rain-dance on anyone who can't answer his questions?"

Straight after Christmas, Mr Barrett was usually on the warpath following the sluggishness of the holidays. He was energised and full of vim and vigour. He almost looked ready to take off as he sailed round the classroom with his black teacher's garb billowing out behind him like a nautical Dracula.

"Look at him," Eoghan thought, eyeing the science teacher cautiously.

Fat Bat practically skipped round on his small feet, moving a desk here and arranging a chair there, making gleeful little remarks and comments as people shuffled in and took their places. He was zipping round the classroom like someone who'd overdosed on Sanatogen. It wasn't such a problem if he kept it all to himself, but he was determined to have all his pupils brimming with zest and energy and enthusiasm too.

"Now let's see how much you have managed to retain during the slothfulness of the Christmas holidays," he chirped. "All the cells in those limited little brains of yours nice and plump and well-fed after your indulgences? Oozing with knowledge and information? Let's find out then, shall we?"

He usually had a New Year science quiz tucked under his arm to get them all jizzed up for the new term. It was based on the work they had done the previous term. Just the thing for after the holidays, he told them happily. And yes, true to form, just squeezing out from his ample upper arm, Eoghan caught a glimpse of a completely squashed quiz. Oh, great, he thought glumly. He couldn't wait.

Sorcha glanced round the class from her seat in the front row. She felt a bit nervous with this teacher, who was like someone let out for the day, dancing round in front of her. There were a couple of others in the front row, but they looked like very serious students who enjoyed a challenge. Eoghan saw her looking round anxiously and he felt a bit sorry for her. Not so sorry that he'd offer to swop, but just a tiny twinge of sympathy that was gone in a second. He found himself distracted by her. She was a bit of all right, he admitted to himself. She had this gorgeous hair, real dark and glossy, cut short with a little lock in front of each ear. There was this squeaky-clean look about her as if she'd just stepped out of the shower. Her face was all pink and shiny.

Maybe it was because she had no make-up on, he mused. Usually, the girls in his class had eyes on them like they'd done a few rounds with Mike Tyson because of all the stuff they plastered on. And they had skin that looked like the pages of some of the crumbly old books in the school library – the ones you had to ask special permission to look at because they were so ancient there was a risk they might fall apart. Eoghan thought they probably used make-up to create the yellow-paper look. It was most likely what they were supposed to look like this year. Eoghan was never too sure what girls were up to with the paint pots they dabbled in all the time. He thought they looked like the living dead.

He glanced sideways.

Take Mary-Anne, he thought. She had all this black stuff caked around her eyelashes that made them stiff and spiky. Then she had kind of a powder on her eyelids – sort of greenish-yellow with a bit of pink at the edges. Eoghan squinted a bit closer. Hang on, he thought. Maybe it wasn't make-up at all.

75

"What are you staring at?" Mary-Anne hissed at him.

"Have you an eye infection?" Eoghan asked, leaning towards her and peering at her eyelids.

"Drop dead! I'll give you something wrong with *your* eyes in a minute and it won't be an infection."

Fat Bat's voice purred pleasantly from the top of the classroom. "Well, I must admit that I missed the entertainment of my maverick back row during the holidays. I can see you have reduced in number; perhaps your third recruit has seen the folly of her ways and has declined to take up her seat this term."

He glanced round the class until he spotted Katie sitting on her own near the window. Katie had been making a great effort in class ever since the little incident with Mr Barrett before Christmas. She still had lunch and hung round with Mary-Anne and Eoghan, and she sat with them in all the other classes. But, in Mr Barrett's class, she told them she had to sit apart from them in case she got into more trouble. Mary-Anne and Eoghan hadn't been too impressed.

"You'd think *we* were the ones who caused the trouble," Mary-Anne said petulantly.

"Yes," agreed Eoghan, pulling a face at Katie.

"You'd think *we* were the ones who'd sent the note in the first place." Mary-Anne continued.

"Yes," agreed Eoghan, tossing his head in the air.

"But we had nothing to do with you getting caught, had we, Eoghan?" said Mary-Anne.

"Yes," said Eoghan, putting his hands on his hips.

"It's 'no' this time," Mary-Anne hissed at him, giving him a puck in the stomach.

Eoghan spluttered a bewildered "no", but it didn't sound very convincing.

In the end, what they said didn't make any difference. Katie just sat away from them anyway.

Mary-Anne scowled now at Eoghan, mad that they'd been caught talking. "Just shut up, Eoghan. Right?"

Fat Bat tutted in surprise. "A little civil war, eh? Well, we'll nip it in the bud immediately. Eoghan, why don't you do the honours and come up here to the front where you can take part in the goings-on of the class? I'm sure we can fit an extra desk along the front here."

"Oh, no, Mr Barrett," moaned Eoghan. "I'm fine back here. Honest."

But Mr Barrett wasn't in the mood for a debate. Gazing up at the ceiling and ignoring Eoghan's pleas, he beckoned him to the top with one hand and, with the other hand, indicated a space of about six inches wide where he expected Eoghan to fit himself, a desk and a chair.

While Eoghan made a big deal of clambering out of his chair and grumbling loudly, picking up his pens and gathering his books and copies, Mary-Anne whispered to him.

"You can impress the new girl and show her how it's done in the front row!" she chuckled wickedly.

There was a bit of shuffling and scraping of desks

until Eoghan got himself wedged firmly in the front row, all escape routes blocked. It was awful. Not only was he now right under Fat Bat's hooter, ready to be hopped on for any question but, because he was in the front, he couldn't slouch down or stretch out his long legs for fear of tripping up his teacher. He had to sit up straight in the chair, with his legs cramped beneath him.

Once the attention had moved off him a bit and Mr Barrett began to get into his teaching stride, Eoghan had a look around him. There, right beside him, sat Sorcha.

"Hi," Eoghan nodded at her.

She smiled back. "I'm Sorcha," she whispered to him.

"What are you sorry for?" he asked, leaning across to hear her better.

"No, I'm *Sorcha*," she repeated. "That's my name."

"Oh, right," he said. "I'm Eoghan."

Now that they had been introduced, Eoghan felt a certain sense of responsibility for Sorcha. After all, he'd been through these quizzes before and he knew what delights faced her. He considered it his role to show her the ropes, to demonstrate how things were done around here, so to speak. She didn't seem to know anyone else and he was going to look after her, he decided.

He really put some genuine effort into the class – more than he'd ever done before. He had his hand up for every question, even though he didn't understand most of them. He was trying so hard that, on one occasion, he nearly knocked Fat Bat's eye out as he shot his hand up.

That caused Sorcha to laugh, which pleased Eoghan no end.

By the end of the lesson, he was exhausted. He'd worked his brain harder than ever before and was now drained. Never before had he put his hand up for so many questions. Even Fat Bat was amazed.

"Well, Eoghan," he said. "It just goes to show what putting you in the front row can do. We must try this more often; it's looking good for the rest of the year if today's class is a measure of the effort you're going to put in. And you never know, you might even get one right next time."

Eoghan grinned self-consciously, aware of Sorcha watching him.

"Thanks, sir," he muttered.

Mary-Anne caught up with Eoghan as he was leaving the classroom. "So, have you cooled down a bit after the heat of that session?"

He looked at her. "What?" he asked, glancing back to see where Sorcha was. She was still at her desk, gathering up her books.

"Somebody has the hots for the new girl and it certainly isn't me! There was practically steam coming out of your ears every time you looked at her," Mary-Anne went on, winding him up.

"Feck off," Eoghan replied. "She just needs a bit of looking out for."

He glanced back again to see Sorcha looking round with uncertainty. It was lunch-time and she probably didn't know where to go for lunch or who to have it with.

"Go on," Katie chirped, joining them at the classroom door. "Why not be her knight in shining armour and gallop to her rescue, Eoghan? You're just the kind of help she needs right now."

"Get off my back," Eoghan snapped. Then, ignoring them further, he pushed his way back through the other pupils coming out and returned to where Sorcha was standing.

"Hi again," he began.

She looked up at him and smiled. "Hi, Eoghan."

"Do you want to join us for lunch?" He gestured to where Mary-Anne and Katie were standing watching him from the door, grinning broadly. Sorcha looked towards them at the door.

"Would your friends mind?" she asked.

"Not at all," Eoghan assured her. "They suggested it."

At the lunch-break, Ciara left the double French class she'd just had and made her way on her own to the canteen where she queued up for coffee at the counter. As she stood there, she glanced round the canteen, trying to spot some familiar faces from her class so that she could join them.

The boys and girls in her year were a decent enough bunch, or so it seemed.

But then, Ciara couldn't really judge because she'd hardly had a chance to talk to them outside of the classroom. They always seemed so *busy*. Galloping off to camogie matches, or scooting off to find someone from the music society, or finishing off the last piece of their homework. Every single one of them had about a hundred things to do during the school day in addition to their ordinary lessons.

There was the library club and the music society that each had meetings twice a week. The school orchestra practised on lunch-times on a Wednesday and also on Thursday after school. A French group was preparing a play about the French revolution to put on during Social Justice Week. Not to mention camogie and hurling, which half the school seemed fanatical about. Then there were the photographic group and the athletics society. Ciara's head was in a whirl just trying to remember all the activities going on. And it appeared that every person in her class was a member of at least two school societies. Christian's Secondary was big into keeping everyone busy at every available minute of the day. It was no wonder the others in her class scarcely had a chance to give her the time of day, let alone sit down and talk about . . . anything. Sure, they'd say "Hi" in the mornings and stuff like that, but that was about it. It just seemed like they didn't have room to squeeze another person into their lives.

It was hardly surprising that Sorcha had been making a song and dance about the difficult job of meeting new people and getting to know the routine in a new school.

Collecting her mug and filling it with coffee from the

machine, Ciara felt a bit grumpy. She could identify exactly with her sister. She missed having her mates to sit with over lunch and to walk with between classes. For the last few days, she'd been eating her lunch on her own in the canteen and having to find her way between classes herself.

Glancing over towards a table by the door, she spotted three people from her class.

"OK," Ciara told herself. "This is it. Go right over there, introduce yourself and join them for lunch. You have to make an effort."

Picking up her steaming mug of coffee and holding her bag of sandwiches, she weaved her way through the throngs of students queuing for drinks and arrived at the table where the three were eating their sandwiches.

"Hi," began Ciara. "Mind if I join you? I'm Ciara, by the way."

"Sit down," one of the girls replied, pulling out a stool from beneath the table for Ciara to sit on. "I'm Cathy, and this is Maria and Úna."

The other two girls nodded and smiled at Ciara.

"Aren't you the new girl in our class?" Maria asked. "I haven't had a chance to talk to you at all – I've been so busy with the school orchestra. We have a *feis* coming up next Friday and we've been squashing in extra practices all over the place."

"Have you managed to find a replacement to play my cello part yet?" Úna asked. "Who'd have thought the *feis* would clash with the camogie finals? I just can't leave them in the lurch – we have to win this year."

"Oh, that's just great," replied Maria. "So you leave us in the lurch to run round a camogie field instead? It's easy to see where your loyalties lie. When there's a choice to be made, the orchestra goes by the board."

"There's no way I'm missing out on the camogie finals. We'll be bringing home the cup this year," said Úna brightly. "So, did you get any cello players to step into my place?"

"Some little beginner from first year has arrived in and is trying to play the part," Maria replied. "But he's hopeless. He keeps getting lost and missing his entries."

"What time is it?" Cathy interrupted them.

Maria looked at her watch. "Oh, my God, it's ten past one! I was supposed to be in the hall for a practice at one. Got to go. See you."

With that, she picked up her violin case from beneath the table and was gone.

Cathy stood up too. "There's a meeting of the library club at one-fifteen. I want to collect my book from the classroom first. Talk to you again, Ciara."

She buzzed off too, leaving Ciara and Úna. Úna finished her mouthful of crisps and began gathering up her bits and pieces.

"Sorry about this," she smiled apologetically at Ciara. "It's nothing personal, but I've a camogie session at one-fifteen. Maybe we'll get to talk some other time."

She was up and off too.

"Sure," said Ciara. "Maybe after about five years somebody will have time to talk to me."

Sitting at an empty table, Ciara felt disgruntled about it all. No wonder Sorcha had been unhappy about changing schools. She'd known what was coming. Sorcha was always more up on things like that than Ciara.

"I never really think through stuff like that," Ciara told herself.

She knew that she just made decisions based on what was best for her swimming; best for her competitions and training, best for her race times.

Maybe Sorcha is right, Ciara thought as she gloomily poured some milk from the jug on the table into her coffee and stirred it. Maybe she needed to get a life. Sorcha was always giving out to her for being too much into her swimming. And now it had landed her in a new school with no friends and no one to chat to.

Getting up from the table, she decided to try and find Sorcha and sit with her during lunch. Generally speaking, the two sisters did their own thing during the school day – mixing with their own year groups and sticking to their own classes, but Ciara decided today was the exception. It was about time she swallowed her pride and told Sorcha that she too was miserable. Sure, it was a dream come true for her swimming and her training. She could get to all of the training sessions no problem and was already knocking seconds off her personal bests, but she had to tell Sorcha that swimming wasn't the only important thing.

Changing schools *was* a bummer.

Ciara knew that Sorcha would get a kick out of hearing that she'd been right all along and that Ciara was prepared to admit that she'd been wrong. Pleased to have made the decision, Ciara headed off to locate the transition year lunch-room which was located in Senior House across the school yard. The lunch-room was just inside the main door of the building. As Ciara pushed open the door, she was greeted by loud peals of Sorcha's laughter sailing down the length of the long narrow room. At the far end of the otherwise empty room, opposite the door, a table had been pushed against the wall and there, sitting on the table with her feet resting on a chair, sat Sorcha. There were three people sitting with her – one tall guy sitting on the table beside her and two girls sitting on chairs pulled alongside the table. They were all doubled over, cracking up at some joke or other, Sorcha included. Their shrieks of laughter echoed round the otherwise empty room. Coffee circles marked the tables that were scattered round and crumbs and crisp bags littered the floor. When they had caught their breath, Sorcha piped up "And you should have seen the way he dived in!" Leaping to her feet and hopping right up on the table, she began demonstrating a parody of an appalling belly-flop dive from the edge of the table while her new friends looked on with delight.

Ciara stared in amazement at the sister she had thought was struggling to make friends in school. Here she was, holding court with a group of mates.

Lonely? Unhappy? Not Sorcha. She looked as if she was in her element, entertaining others with her antics. Suddenly feeling a bit foolish and unhappier than ever, Ciara watched her for a moment or two longer. Then, not wishing to be seen, she slipped quietly back through the door and returned to her own canteen for lunch.

Chapter 7

Five o'clock on Wednesday evening.

Ciara had already finished the warm-up for her evening training. She climbed out of the pool with the other swimmers when Mark blew his whistle.

"OK, can everybody hear me? Settle down, please."

Fifteen swimmers gathered round where Mark stood on the bank. Most of them propped themselves against the diving blocks that were lined up on the poolside, their arms folded across their chests. Some of them stayed in the pool, dipping up and down in the water's rhythmic movement, their hands gripping the rails, the sides of their swim-hats turned up above their ears to hear better. Others were sitting on the tiled poolside, their feet dipping in the water.

"Right," Mark went on when he was sure he had everyone's attention. "This is our last evening training session before the Silver Fish meet." There was a little ripple of nervous chatter and laughter that ran round his group of competitive swimmers. "As you know, tomorrow's and Friday's swimming sessions – both mornings and evenings – are out of bounds for you lot. No training. Take it easy. Rest a bit at home."

"I'd prefer to get into the pool and do a few lengths, Mark. Just warm up my muscles, you know, even for half an hour or so," one of the boys called out.

"No way, Dónal." Mark was insistent. "I really want you to force your bodies to rest. You've done all the training. Improved your times. Built up your stamina. Worked on technique. You have two days left before a major competition in a fifty-metre pool and I want you to ease off on yourselves. Don't stress your bodies." He drew his hands through the air in a long, slow movement to emphasise his point. "You'll be putting yourselves through enough strain over the weekend and you need to conserve a bit of energy."

"What about this session?" somebody asked. "Will it be heavy training?"

"We'll be working on starts and turns for most of the time after the warm-up," Mark replied. "I'll get on to that in a minute. Let me finish first about the meet."

He went on to give the swimmers details about their own competition times. He also told them the times of the warm-up sessions when the main pool was available for competitors to do a few lengths and get the feel of the water, a sense of the lanes.

"For those of you who haven't been to Manchester before," he explained, "there's a combined swim-down pool adjacent to the main pool. That's a smaller pool for you to warm up before your event and to cool down afterwards. Make sure you use it. It's there for all the competitors so it's OK to spend a bit of time there. I'll give you the specific times it's available for the various events. There's also a wide deck space and spectator area with seating for over five hundred so there'll be lots of people milling around. Don't let that put you off. We're arriving early on the day to give you all a chance to look around the place and get used to it."

Those swimmers who hadn't been to Manchester before looked at each other nervously. A fifty-metre pool? Some of them had never even seen a fifty-metre pool in real life before, never mind swum in one. The idea of having a specially-made swim-down pool, a massive spectator area and a broad pool deck was mind-blowing, compared to the twenty-five-metre pool in which they trained. That had seating at one end of it for about fifty people seated on plastic stacking chairs that were stored in a lock-up room and taken out for galas. The rest of the narrow pool area was out of bounds during competitions in case any unfortunate spectator went for a nosedive into the water. And there was certainly no swim-down pool. The pool at Manchester was in a different league.

"Oh, my God," one of the younger competitors cried nervously. "How am I ever going to get through it all?" The more experienced swimmers grinned.

Mark smiled briefly. "Relax, that's the key. And focus your mind on your swimming. You'll be fine. I wouldn't have put any of you into this competition if I didn't think you'd be OK."

Ciara listened intently from where she sat on a

stack of polystyrene swim-boards. She knew it was one of the biggest things that threw a swimmer off on the day of a competition: the strangeness of the venue. A big pool, a crowded spectator gallery, a different feel to the water, unfamiliar sounds and smells, new changing rooms . . . if a swimmer was all keyed up and twitchy, an unfamiliar competition venue could really throw them off.

But she felt OK about this competition.

She knew she was ready.

It was now mid-February – almost six weeks since she'd started cycling to early morning training from her gran's house. She was progressing steadily though Mark's programme and felt strong and fit, a good way to be before a competition. Positive mental attitude: Mark was always going on about it and now Ciara really understood what he meant. For the first time, she felt that she'd worked though an all-over training programme designed specially for her – her speed and times were good. For the most part, her technique was fine although her back-stroke in the Individual Medley tended to be a bit choppy, especially if she was tense. But if she could keep her head in the 400-metre IM she stood a good chance of a gold.

The Silver Fish was generally used by Mark as a preliminary gauge of a how a swimmer would perform in the national championships. He wasn't too concerned if his swimmers didn't bring home a scoop of medals. He concentrated more on their performance on the day.

He checked out what fazed them, how their style altered in competition, if their stroke count changed much when under pressure. Then he used the information to inform their training schedules for the Leinsters in April and finally, the nationals in June.

The Silver Fish meet in Manchester three years previously had been Ciara's first competition outside Ireland. She'd been only eleven years old so she knew exactly how wound up the younger swimmers felt now. She'd been sick with nerves for a week before the competition. The sight of the huge pool and the massive sports complex in which it was located had completely freaked her: so much so that it was all she could do to get through her events in one piece. Forget the semis and the finals – the heats were as far as she got. Her personal bests went out the window. Her technique couldn't have been worse. Her thinking was all over the place. But it was all for experience.

It was the same for these young swimmers now. Most of them were just going for the experience of being at an international meet. If they got some major competition under their belts, out of the way, then they'd be useful and ready to compete next time round.

". . . so try to bulk up on high-carbohydrate foods before and after your competitions and within an hour of finishing your warm-ups. Pack a bag with snacks to munch on to keep your sugar levels at a peak," Mark instructed them.

"What about my teeth?" someone joked. "I'll be a great swimmer but I'll have no teeth."

Mark smiled. "Pack a toothbrush, too, and chew on it regularly!"

"What kind of snacks do we bring? Chocolate and Mars Bars?"

"No, no. Too heavy. Pack some bags of popcorn, scones, pots of low-fat yoghurt. Maybe a few bags of jelly babies, some biscuits, a couple of cartons of fruit juice. That kind of stuff."

"And the kitchen sink while you're at it," someone piped up.

When they'd finished going through the travel plans for Saturday, Mark was keen to get them into the water. It was by then five-fifteen.

"I don't want any of you catching a chill. We'll do a few lengths to warm up the muscles a bit and then work on starts and turns going across the pool."

They divided themselves among the lanes and began diving in at each pip of the whistle. Mark watched them as they cut up and down the pool. He counted them as they passed by where he stood . . . fourteen, fifteen . . . "Hold on," he thought.

There should be sixteen. Sixteen competitors. He checked his list of competitors. Sixteen swimmers were booked for the gala. Sixteen swimmers had qualified for their events and this was their last swim before the competition. His last chance as their trainer to ease any ragged nerves, to go through the routine. But there were only fifteen swimmers in the pool. And only fifteen swimmers had listened to his briefing and knew all the details.

Who was missing?

What swimmer had failed to show up to such an important training session?

"What time is it?" Sorcha asked Eoghan.

They were all sitting together in the spectator gallery of the snooker hall. Sorcha had started going round to the hall with Mary-Anne, Katie and Eoghan after school.

The spectator gallery was a rather grand name for a double row of wooden fold-down seats that were screwed to the base of a rostrum raised about two feet above the floor level of the hall. It doubled as a general hanging-around area where groups of boys and girls ate chips, drank Coke and chatted, and as a waiting area for young players who were queuing for snooker tables. The waiting players had signed up at their table of choice and they sat idly chatting, watching their friends finishing off their games. The single light above each of the eight snooker tables in the hall illuminated the green baize and the polished coloured balls.

At the far end of the hall, a row of about twenty one-armed bandits, pinball machines, slot machines and vending machines jangled and rattled and flashed their coloured lights as they swallowed up loose change. Their brightness and garishness wiped out any professional snooker hall atmosphere. The place was solely a hang-out for young people after school. And sometimes during school, too, if things were too tough to handle. Those from ten years old to twenty pitted their wits against the one-armed bandits, walking from machine to machine depending on the money in their pockets and what games they most enjoyed.

Apart from the table lights and the rows of coloured bulbs on the machines, the hall was unlit. Its dimness made it all the better. It gave it a late-night clubby feel so it was a cool place to hang out. The low light also hid the scruffiness – the stained floor and the graffiti-covered walls. In the darkness, all that was missing was the hush of competition, the pall of thick smoke lingering in the air and the smart suits of the professional snooker players as they paced round the tables. But it wasn't too difficult to imagine.

"I don't know. Can't see my watch," Eoghan replied.

"What do you want to know for?" Mary-Anne asked her. "It's still early."

"I shouldn't be here," Sorcha replied.

"Nor should I. My father'd freak if he saw me. He thinks this place is a hotbed of drugs and low life." Katie said.

"So what?" Eoghan asked her.

"I'm supposed to be swimming at five," Sorcha replied.

"Swimming!" Eoghan snorted. "This is better *craic* than swimming any day."

Sorcha straightened her back and stretched. "I know. But there's no rest for the wicked."

She took hold of Eoghan's wrist and twisted it towards the light from the nearest snooker table until his watch face was illuminated.

"Dammit, anyway," she muttered. "It's five-fifteen. I'm already late."

She turned and looked at them. "I should go." But she didn't make any move to leave.

"Don't bother," Eoghan told her. "They won't miss you."

"Why don't the two of you make yourselves useful and get us all some food instead?" Mary-Anne grinned at them. "I'm starving and it'll take your mind off the swimming thing."

"I was wondering what was wrong with my stomach," Eoghan said, rubbing it. "I'm hungry! Come on, Sorcha, let's go."

After Mary-Anne and Katie groped in the dark to find the right money and hand it over, Sorcha and Eoghan strolled to the chipper to order chips and batter burgers. It was raining; a cold, wet, February evening.

"We'll have to run for it," Sorcha said, wrapping her cardigan around her. They legged it though the teeming rain and into the chipper. A delicious smell of hot chips and burgers greeted them as they opened the door and went in. The windows were steamed up from the heat and the damp. While they waited for their order, Sorcha wrote her name with her finger on the misted window. Eoghan watched her. When she'd finished, he wrote his initials beneath her name and encircled it with a big heart. He wasn't very good at drawing and the heart rubbed out part of Sorcha's name and wobbled a bit on one side. But it was still recognisable. Sorcha stared at it, not sure what to say, and then giggled with unease.

"Eoghan!" she said to him. "What are you doing?"

She pulled her cardigan sleeve over her hand and rubbed it across the window, erasing the drawing. Eoghan got embarrassed by her reaction and pretended to be fascinated by the menu hanging on the wall of the chipper. He read aloud.

"Batter burger, batter pineapple, batter sausages, curry sauce and chips . . ."

"I should have gone swimming," Sorcha said flatly, rubbing her damp sleeve dry and looking up at him. "I'm in a competition in Manchester on Saturday. I should have gone training tonight."

"Missing tonight won't change things," Eoghan reasoned. "I miss a lot of football training but my team still won the league last year."

Sorcha looked at him. "Except it's not just tonight. This is the fourth session I've missed recently. Mark'll probably chuck me out of the gala now. Never mind the club."

Their order arrived and they paid for the paper bags of food.

"I'll go to the pool after this," Sorcha told Eoghan. "I need to talk to Mark."

"I'll walk you there," Eoghan told her. The words were out before he had time to think of what she might say, particularly given that she had rubbed out his love-heart. That was still smarting with him.

Sorcha paused for a moment, thinking also of the heart on the steamed-up window. "Don't go out of your way especially for me," she said, blushing. She glanced quickly at him.

"I don't mind," Eoghan replied as they went back to the snooker hall. He tried to think of something alluring to follow up with, but only managed, "I want to."

By quarter to six, Mark knew that Sorcha had no intention of turning up for training. Now what to do? he wondered to himself. He scanned her events to see whether he should pull her out of the competition altogether. She had qualified for three heats – fifty-metre freestyle, 100-metre freestyle and 100-metre 'fly. Good events for Sorcha. She stood a good chance, especially in the fifty free. But he didn't like his other swimmers seeing him allow someone who lacked dedication stay in a competition. He was usually tough but fair. If someone missed the last session before a meet without a reasonable excuse, they were automatically dropped from the gala. In the usual run of things, Sorcha would be disqualified and that was that.

But Mark had to weigh this one up carefully.

If he pulled her out entirely, would Sorcha really care? He didn't think so. In fact, if anything, he thought she'd probably be quite happy about it. She'd been losing interest for a while now. She'd missed several evening sessions recently. When she did make it, her arrival times were sloppy. And she generally only got to two morning sessions a week.

It often happened at her age. Other things in her life had taken over – friends, schools, boys. It wasn't really surprising, but it was disappointing given that Sorcha could be a good swimmer. She had an edge about her, a neat style that enabled her to cut through the short distances efficiently. But she lacked ambition. Drive. Guts.

Mark looked down to where Ciara was training. They had taken up the ropes dividing the lanes and were working on turns against the wall of the pool. She was practising her IM turns. From butterfly to backstroke. From backstroke to breast. To front crawl. Again and again. Over and back across the width of the pool. Swim, turn, swim, turn. She was good. Not only that, she was determined to make it. That was half the battle.

It occurred to Mark that pulling Sorcha from the competition this coming weekend might have more of an impact on Ciara than on Sorcha. Ciara was a fantastic swimmer but she could be thrown off balance if she was edgy. She could be a bit brittle in the face of competition and she might respond badly to the hassle of Sorcha being disqualified. Ciara's training had been going smoothly for the past six or eight weeks. She was on track for a great season. It was important to maintain some equilibrium for her. Maybe leaving Sorcha in the Silver Fish this weekend would prove to be an advantage to Ciara; maintain the *status quo*. The two sisters would be travelling together and Ciara was accustomed to the routine. Pulling Sorcha from the gala might upset Ciara. Maybe, on this occasion, Mark would relax his unwritten rule of no show, no go. And deal with any disgruntled swimmers after the event.

Chapter 8

When the evening training session was over, Ciara showered and changed. Once dressed, she made her way out of the changing rooms and headed up to collect her bike from the storeroom. But it wasn't there. Martha must have had to move it out of the store for a delivery of chemicals. Ciara was on her way back through the office when she met Martha.

"Have you seen my bike?" Ciara asked.

"Your parents have it," Martha replied.

"My parents?" How did her parents get her bike? They were eight miles away at home and not due round to her granny's house until later on that night.

"They arrived here about fifteen minutes ago to collect you. You were just getting out of the pool at the time. They've put your bike in the boot of the car and they're waiting outside to give you a lift."

"Way to go!" said Ciara with delight. "A lift home on a mucky evening. Excellent! See you, Martha."

With that, Ciara ran out of the building and across the rain-splashed carpark to where her parents sat in the car. She opened the back door and sat in.

"Hi!" she began. "This is brilliant. I won't get wet again going home. I wasn't expecting to see either of you until later tonight."

"We thought we'd collect both of you and have another look at the new house. We finished the final paperwork this afternoon and should get the keys this weekend," her father smiled at her.

"That's great news. I think it's the best of the ones we've looked at," Ciara replied. "It's the nearest to the pool anyway."

"And it has that lovely big back garden," her mother smiled.

Ciara was excited. They'd been to look at lots of houses over the last few weekends, but the one they had finally secured seemed to have what everybody wanted – a room for each of the girls, near to the pool and school, a big garden, a spare bedroom. Granny's was fine, but she was looking forward to moving back into her own place with her mum and dad and Sorcha. Their parents called round every night and Granny was a pet, but it still wasn't *home* or her family's routine.

Her mother continued. "We've already called round and told your grandmother. She knows that we're bringing you round to the house and not to expect you home immediately. Where's Sorcha? Her bike wasn't in the hall."

Ciara's face fell. She knew her parents weren't aware that Sorcha hadn't really been keeping to her swimming routine. Sorcha glossed over the subject lightly when they asked, not saying anything too specific and generally agreeing with Ciara's comments.

And Ciara certainly hadn't said anything to her parents. Well, what could she say? She was hardly going to sit them down and fill them in on a few facts about her sister. Hey, Mum and Dad, don't you realise that Sorcha couldn't be bothered with all this swimming stuff? She's much more into snooker halls and hanging out with her friends. Haven't you noticed her resistance to any increase in training times or pressure of competitions? And have you happened to pick up the smell of cigarettes and chips from her clothes, by any chance? Sorcha had been losing interest in swimming long before they changed schools, but now, with the attraction of new friends, and no parents around to bring her to and from the pool each day, Sorcha was making the most of her new-found freedom – making her mark in Christian's Secondary.

It had taken Ciara a while to see what was happening. Even though she lived with Sorcha, even though they went to the same school, Ciara hadn't really wised up to where Sorcha was until that day she stumbled in on her entertaining her mates in the transition year lunch-room. She'd seen Sorcha in her own world then. At her best.

Entertaining.

The centre of attention.

Loving the drama.

It was like the blinkers had been removed from Ciara's eyes. All the stuff Sorcha had been saying about

Ciara messing up her life, about needing to learn to chill out, to live properly and not only focus on swimming: Sorcha had really been talking about herself. In a kind of obscure way, she was telling Ciara that she, Sorcha, wasn't going to mess her life up by only having swimming as her passion. But Ciara had only heard the words, not really understood their meaning. It was like talking in code but Ciara had only cracked the code recently. *Her* natural element was water. Her environment was the pool. Her thing was swimming. But Sorcha had another habitat where she was comfortable. Maybe it wasn't too clear yet what that was, but it certainly wasn't the pool and competitive swimming. It was gutsier and far more interesting than swimming, Sorcha thought. It was real life.

How could Ciara expect her parents to notice all this? They were caught up in moving house and sorting out a new school for their daughters. How could they notice something that Ciara, who probably knew Sorcha better than anyone, had only copped on to lately?

This time round, there was no hiding it. Sorcha was not at the swimming-pool and her parents were wondering where she was.

"She didn't make it down this evening," Ciara said.

"Why ever not?" her mother asked.

Ciara wasn't sure what to say *to that one*. Why not? She didn't know *exactly* why not, but she could hazard a fair guess at it. For crying out loud, she was Sorcha's sister, after all, not her baby-sitter. New friends in Christian's Secondary were taking up more and more of her time. Particularly this group of three who had a reputation for being right messers. Ciara had heard that the guy, in particular, was close to being expelled. And his pals weren't much better; real losers. Trust Sorcha to take up with them, of all people.

"I think she had something else on," Ciara said lamely. "Something came up at the last moment."

It was pretty obvious that she was making excuses. And not very good ones at that.

"Like what?" her father asked, his voice slightly harder. "She knows her routine. We were round with you both in Gran's last night and she never mentioned anything else being on today." He turned to his wife. "Did she ask you about going to something else?"

"Certainly not," she replied. "In fact, she was talking about tonight being the last training session before the Silver Fish. Am I right, Ciara?"

"Tonight was the last session before the meet," Ciara agreed.

"We can't leave until she gets here – that's assuming she's coming at all. Maybe she's gone straight to Gran's," her mother continued.

"We'll give her five minutes then drive round and see," said her dad. "It's a pity something happened to make her miss her swimming. I hope it's nothing serious."

They sat in silence. Ciara wasn't too sure what to say. She knew a fair bit about the exploits of Sorcha's new friends. They'd been caught smoking in the school and were well-known for mitching. They drank a fair bit at weekends, too. And the boy, he'd been found in the girls' cloakroom hiding among the coats when a gym class had been changing and had a reputation for trying it on with anyone in a skirt. He was on his last chance before being suspended. But that was Sorcha for you, Ciara sighed, anything with a bit of excitement and she was away.

She sat in the car now and listened to the fat rain pattering heavily on the car roof. Her parents looked straight ahead at the raindrops splattering on the windscreen.

"Look at the weather! It's rotten. I'm going to get soaked," Sorcha griped as they emerged from the snooker hall. "I don't even have a coat with me."

It was dark now.

Eoghan belched as he came out behind Sorcha and rubbed his stomach. "I shouldn't have had that curry sauce on my chips. It's going to be repeating on me all night."

"Come on," said Sorcha. "I'm going up to the pool. Are you coming?"

"I am," Eoghan replied. "Did I tell you I can't swim? My older brother tried to feed me to the crabs on Cahore Strand when I was a nipper and, only my mam saved me, I'd have been a goner. Can't look at the water since." He grinned at Sorcha. "Except for my bath on a Friday night of course."

"You wait here," Sorcha told him as she ran across the wet street to fetch her bike from where it was chained to a lamppost. Eoghan watched her from the porch of the snooker hall. Mary-Anne and Katie came out behind him, buttoning up their jackets.

"What a night," Katie exclaimed, looking up at the teeming rain.

"You behave yourself with that young one," Mary-Anne warned Eoghan, out of Sorcha's earshot.

Eoghan looked at her, his eyes wide. "Me? I'm not going to do anything!"

"Oh, sure. And I'm Elvis Presley. Just don't mess her around, Eoghan. She doesn't know you yet and hasn't a clue what she's letting herself in for."

"I'm only walking her to the pool," Eoghan argued. "That's very innocent."

"Pull the other one, it's got bells on," Mary-Anne said. "Don't forget I know you from experience, Eoghan. The innocence with you lasts less than two shakes of a lamb's tail! It might be innocent this time, but not for long."

"What's this?" Sorcha asked, wheeling her bike over to join them.

"I was just saying 'So long'," Mary-Anne said brightly. "Enjoy yourselves."

"Come on, Sorcha," Eoghan said gruffly as Mary-Anne and Katie walked off in the opposite direction.

"What was that about?" Sorcha asked as they headed towards the pool. She glanced back at Mary-Anne and Katie but they had already disappeared in the rain and darkness.

"Mary-Anne's worse than my mam at harping on about nothing," Eoghan told her, digging his hands deep into his pockets and hunching his shoulders up to protect himself from the rain. He mimicked Mary-Anne's high-pitched voice. "'Eoghan, do this' and 'Eoghan, don't do that.' Does my head in at times."

"You and Mary-Anne go back quite a way, don't you? Katie told me you went out with Mary-Anne last year."

"But that doesn't mean I'm chained to her for life. Someone needs to tell her that."

Sorcha felt a bit uncomfortable. "I don't want to get between you and her if she's still carrying a torch for you. You know what they say about hell having no fury like a woman scorned."

"What are you talking about?" Eoghan stopped and frowned at her. "When did we start talking about torches and hell? I think I missed something there."

Sorcha laughed. "Forget it," she told him as they rambled on.

Vague shadows appeared at the gate into the carpark. As Ciara watched, they became clearer. Walking slowly and wheeling a bicycle between them, two figures strolled through the darkness and rain towards the lit doorway of the swimming-pool. Their reflections danced awkwardly through the puddles, like daddy-long-legs reflected in flashes of neon. Sorcha was wheeling her bike. Walking next to her was Eoghan. She didn't notice her parents' car until she was right beside it and saw Ciara's face peering out of the back window. She stopped abruptly and said something to Eoghan, who looked towards the car also. A few words passed between them. Then he walked back out of the carpark again while Sorcha took her bike and wheeled it round to the rear of the car.

Her father got out of the car immediately as soon as Eoghan had left. "Sorcha," he began. "Where have you been? We've been here . . . " Ciara couldn't hear any more because he slammed the car door. Nor did she hear Sorcha's response. Together, he and Sorcha put the bicycle into the boot, tying the hood of the boot down with rope to hold in the two bikes. Sorcha then opened the back door and sat in beside Ciara. Her school uniform was soaking wet and water streamed from her hair and ran into her eyes. She smiled at Ciara, then turned to her mother.

"Hi, Mum. What a surprise, eh?"

"Where have you been?" her mother asked, turning round. "Look at you. You're drenched. Did you get a puncture?"

"No, I didn't," Sorcha told her. "I was . . . with some friends. We were chatting and I lost track of the time."

Her father sat into the car and started the engine. "Must be a very important friend to make you miss your swimming," he commented. He was not impressed with Sorcha's no show and poor excuse. "I hope he's worth it when Mark pulls you out of the gala this weekend."

Sorcha had forgotten all about needing to go and talk to Mark about the gala.

"Can you hang on a minute while I run in to see Mark? I won't be a second. Can you turn the car or something?"

Her father was getting more annoyed by the minute.

"The car is already turned, Sorcha, and we've been sitting in it waiting for the last fifteen minutes. Hurry up."

"Thanks a million."

Sorcha scooted out of the car, ran across the carpark and into the pool. She was back in five minutes, a slightly puzzled look on her face.

"He's still letting me swim in the gala," she told them. "Just on this occasion, he said."

Her father looked at her reflection in the driver's mirror. "If I had my way, you wouldn't be swimming in it," he told her sternly. "With your fooling around, you don't deserve to be given a chance to swim in any gala."

Chapter 9

The Silver Fish Senior Girls' 400-metre Individual Medley was called at three-fifteen in the afternoon. The pool was massive – stretching out in front of the spectators and competitors. Fifty metres of shining blue water. Eight lanes separated by ropes of red and yellow floats. Its size alone was intimidating, even without having to swim eight lengths of it for the 400-metre IM. Because of the pool's size, each stroke in the Individual Medley was swum over two lengths, starting off with butterfly because it took up the most energy. It was best to get it out of the way first. Back crawl was next, followed by breaststroke. Front crawl, the fastest, was swum last.

Ciara stood at the chair placed at the back pool wall, in front of her lane, limbering up. She felt good. Strong. Her times were low. The extra few hours training every week had had a significant impact on her speeds. She had dropped her personal best not by six seconds, her target, but by a massive eleven seconds. It now stood at 4.56, five seconds faster than the qualifying time for the meet.

She looked to left and right of her as she unzipped her track suit top. The other swimmers were preparing too, taking off their sweatshirts, adjusting their goggles, stretching their limbs to loosen up and as a way of easing taut nerves. She turned towards the pool.

The water was clear and shimmering.

Ciara's stomach felt tight, her ears zinging.

"Hold easy till the last twenty-five," Mark whispered, taking her track suit top from her. She wished now he wasn't beside her, wished he would leave her to gather her thoughts. But he was as anxious as she was, eager to get the last bit of advice in. "Don't burn yourself out on the front hundred, hold back. Let the others do the work. Take up the slack and pace them. Hold your reserves together until your final turn. You have the speed, just pace yourself. And concentrate. Keep your mind on the race."

His breathing was fast, his instructions laconic.

Ciara nodded, fixing her cap around her ears, snapping at the strap on her goggles.

"Swimmers to the blocks, please."

The voice over the loudspeaker system crackled, silencing the spectators.

"Go for it, Ciara," Mark muttered as he moved back behind the barriers around the pool.

Ciara walked over to the blocks, glancing at her opponents. She was well positioned in lane four. The competitors in five of the lanes held no threat for her, little-known swimmers who had just broken through to the finals. They were really just swimming for the experience of it, knowing their times would not match those of the three favourites. It would be good experience for future competitions. Lanes 5 and 6 were the serious ones to watch.

The girl in lane 5 was Rachel Reed, an old rival of Ciara's from her early competition days. Rachel swam for an English club. She had won the heats with the best time overall. Rachel always gave every race her best – even the heats – and still seemed to come out tops. Ciara had watched her swim an impressive time that morning, immediately before her own heat. Rachel was way ahead of the rest, cutting through the water swiftly. Ciara knew it wouldn't have taken a feather out of her. She was strong, did a lot of weights training. She'd be ready for this swim now as though she hadn't swum all day.

Lane 6 was Susan Kiernan – a nifty little swimmer who would be easy to overlook if you didn't know her form. She was small, just over five foot, and unassuming. As usual, Susan just scraped through her heat, the same heat that Rachel had swum, making the finals by only a second. She always tried to get into the last heats if at all possible so that she knew the times she had to beat. Then, with a precision that was uncanny, she made the time by a couple of seconds, pacing her swim to fit. She could pump power into her strokes if she felt she was slowing a little to make up time and then ease off near the end to conserve energy.

"There's a swimmer you have to watch," Mark said of her. "She knows the speed of her own strokes like no one else, can calculate better that a computer. Watch her, Ciara. She'll drift along in your wake, and then, pow! leave you standing on the last length."

"Why does she take such a risk in the heats? I've seen her miss a final because of not doing her best, yet I know she has it in her."

"Look at her. She's small. How could she power through a heat and risk having nothing left for the final? She's not built like you or Rachel, couldn't take the two races in one day without holding back on one of them. Safer to do that in the heats than the final. So she's learnt, knows how to time her strokes. She's been well trained."

Standing on the blocks, Ciara looked down at the water. Oily in its movements, it lapped the edges of the pool.

"Take your marks . . ."

Ciara stepped carefully to the edge of the block, getting her balance.

"Get set . . ."

She tensed herself and crouched over.

"Go!"

At the crack of the gun, Ciara launched herself outwards, stretching long and lean, tracing a shallow arc through the air before skimming the water surface. She cut the water cleanly, its cool silkiness plunging her into a sudden silence and blueness. One, two strong flutter kicks and she surfaced, powering straight into the strong double-overarm of the butterfly, the cheers and splashes abruptly loud and crashing in her ears. She sliced through the water towards the far end of the pool. Her thoughts formed rapidly into a rhythm – kick, pull, kick, pull – breathing only on every second stroke. She viewed her position. Towards the end of her first length, she was holding her own well. Barely a nose in front of the others. She was aware of the swimmer in lane 3 pulling up on her. They were almost neck and neck.

Rachel in lane five wasn't to be seen without Ciara turning her head, a cardinal sin, so she couldn't place her for now. The other lanes were also too far to see without losing rhythm.

Her first turn was good. She made firm contact with the wall and stayed neat and tight. She pushed off strongly into the second length of the butterfly.

Must pull ahead of lane three, Ciara thought. Must begin to break a lead from her. Her efforts worked and she began to edge ahead slowly. This swimmer wasn't such a nobody after all, thought Ciara. She was pulling hard when Mark's words suddenly popped into her head. "Don't burn yourself out in the front hundred, let them take the lead." He was right. She'd have nothing left otherwise. Especially the 'fly, it would exhaust her before the race was quarter over. She had to try and conserve energy for the last length. Susan would be able to beat her otherwise. Ciara eased up, stopped trying to pull ahead of lane three. She resumed her original rhythm, steady, confident.

But her second turn was weak. Her concentration was lost momentarily thinking of Mark's advice. A ragged turn, she missed the wall for a powerful kick-off into the backstroke and lost her place. Suddenly, Rachel appeared at her left shoulder. She was looking good, fresh. She powered alongside Ciara, dipping and peaking in her distinctive backstroke, her downward arm-pull strong and deep. Ciara was determined to stick with her and not let much water between them, but the backstroke wasn't her best and Rachel was a good backstroker. Despite Ciara's best efforts, Rachel pulled slowly ahead, increasing the distance. By the end of the third length, Rachel had built up a good lead. In second place at this stage was the unexpected swimmer in lane three. They were followed very closely by Ciara who held on to third place on the turn into the fourth length.

But only just.

Halfway through the race and Ciara knew her best two strokes were yet to come, but she'd need to do her utmost to close the gap between herself and Rachel. Rachel's best strokes were her backstroke and her crawl. One of those had already been swum, so Ciara's best chances lay in the next fifty metres. The swimmer in lane three was beginning to tire, her impressive start now flagging a little. The other lanes couldn't be seen beyond the churning waters and Ciara had no idea where Susan was.

When Ciara turned into her breaststroke, Rachel had already pushed off. Swinging into her smooth style, Ciara stretched out, determined to close the gap. She could feel herself drawing closer to Rachel. It was between the two of them. Lane three's swimmer had dropped off now, no longer a threat.

On a high lift for breath, Ciara thought she caught a glimpse of Susan's red cap two lanes to her left. She felt a spike of panic in her stomach. Susan's breaststroke was good. Her short length gave her a faster arm pull and a quick recovery. She also had an effective glide, not unlike Sorcha in her neat, fast stroke. Able to gain water quickly, efficiently. Her arm pull was shorter than Ciara's own so she dipped and peaked in the water more frequently.

Ciara knew that Susan would be counting her strokes as she swam; accurate, precise, gauging the best time to power forward. Trying not to get distracted, she ignored the sight of Susan and concentrated on her own stroke. She moved steadily, closing the gap on Rachel, but she could feel herself beginning to tire. The third quarter was tiring, demanding great effort at this stage in the race. At the turn, Rachel was only a hair's-breadth ahead. Ciara's wall-kick brought her alongside Rachel. They paced each other for most of the length, Ciara coming into her turn a whisker ahead of her rival. Turning swiftly into crawl at the wall, Ciara moved into the final leg of the race ahead of Rachel, but still not clear of Susan's position. She knew she could be anywhere – but not far. It was a race between the three of them now, the lesser swimmers having fallen back on the breaststroke, their lack of stamina now showing.

The front length of the crawl was slow, with little change in the positions. They were all weary now. It was plain to see. The advantage would go to those who had managed to hold back and conserve some energy, those who had not burnt themselves out in the opening stages. Ciara stopped pushing herself to the utmost, maintaining her lead on Rachel but trying to conserve her energy for the final length. She drew breath at one stage and was alarmed to see the lift of Susan's elbow across from her. But Ciara's height would give her the advantage on the turn. She had to make sure she timed it well to make the most of the push-off coming into the final stretch.

The wall loomed ahead and Ciara curled in her right arm, swinging her legs round at the last moment and clamping her feet firmly against the tiled surface. She pushed off powerfully, supplementing her kick with an arm-pull, and cut into the last length. She was abruptly aware of cheers and yells from the spectators but didn't know who they were for. Maybe she was in the lead. It would be wonderful if she managed to make it in first. To scoop a gold on the Silver Fish would bode well for the season: start everything on a high note after a winter of hard training.

Rachel was close to her, powering along, but Ciara put her all into this final twenty-five. Her muscles were aching now, her breathing coming in ragged gulps, not the steady inhale, exhale of the earlier part of the race. Even so, she knew she was doing a good pace, could feel herself cutting through the water. A flicker of movement over her shoulder startled her. Rachel was drawing on reserves of energy that Ciara knew she didn't have herself; seeking to gain the lead on Ciara again, to inch ahead that vital distance that would make a difference. Ciara kept her rhythm, trying desperately to push even more energy from her exhausted muscles. But she was pretty much burnt out. Everything was going into maintaining her pace. There was nothing more to give.

She could see the final wall, hear the crescendo of shouts.

Don't slow up, she told herself. Keep up the rhythm right to the end. "Hit that wall with impact," Mark's words echoed in her head. "Smash your way through it, but don't stop." Ciara swam on until her reaching hand slapped against tiles and she pulled up, lifting her head to see her rivals.

Rachel was touching at that point, just after Ciara. But Susan? Ciara swung around to see. Susan had pulled up too, and was looking over at Ciara. Neither knew who had won. The other swimmers had come in by the time the times went up on the board. Lane six was displayed first, Susan's lane: four minutes, fifty-eight seconds. A very good time. The times for the inexperienced swimmers came up next: all of them well over five minutes and ten seconds. Rachel's time went up, she'd swum a reasonable time: five minutes, one second. Not good enough, however. She wouldn't be pleased with that time. And lane 2? What about Ciara's own time?

It appeared.

Four minutes, fifty-nine seconds.

Ciara was a second behind Susan.

She hadn't won.

She was in second place.

Ciara stared at the board in disbelief.

Three seconds slower than her personal best. *Three* whole seconds!

The first competition of the season. She was beaten by a second and she was three seconds slower than she was able to do.

Ciara felt gutted with disappointment. Her eyes pricked with tears that she furiously blinked back.

A cheer went up from the spectators as each of the swimmers congratulated the others. Ciara and Rachel both swam over and shook Susan's hand, as did the other swimmers from the race. It was a good win – a whole second. They finished congratulating each other before climbing out of the pool. The pool attendants began positioning the diving blocks for the next race, while timekeepers noted the recorded times on their time sheets and reset their watches.

Ciara walked over to her chair. Unzipping her kit-bag, she pulled out a towel. She put on her track suit top over her swimsuit.

"Well done, Ciara. You were great!" Sorcha appeared at her side, patting her shoulder. "I knew you'd beat Rachel. Susan came up like a tornado for the last length. I'm sure you could hear the shrieks of excitement. There's no way you could have anticipated it. A silver medal, a good start to the season."

Ciara forced a smile. "Thank you. Not a good time though, Sorcha. I was terrible."

"Come on!" Sorcha cried. "It's your first competition of the season. Give yourself a break."

Ciara looked at her sister. Sorcha was dressed after her own race, her short, damp hair sticking out all over the place like a little hedgehog. Ciara tried to shake herself from her disappointment by asking Sorcha about her own swim. "What about you? How did your heat go?"

Sorcha shrugged. "I blew it. Hardly surprising, given my training routine over the last while."

Ciara was disappointed for her sister. But she was pleased that she'd made it to the gala, all the same, glad she was there to talk to now.

"I didn't get to see you," Ciara said. "My own heat had just finished."

"You missed nothing exciting. Don't worry."

"When's your next event?"

"The 100 'fly is this afternoon. Maybe I'll come up trumps in that."

Ciara nodded encouragingly. "You'll beat the socks off them."

"I wouldn't put any money on it."

Mark joined them at the pool end. "Good race, Ciara." He shook her hand solemnly. His eyes were serious, studying Ciara's face carefully. "A well-deserved silver. It's the beginning of the season," he told her. "Your first event. You can only get better from here. You're in great shape."

Ciara looked at him and shrugged. "Thank you."

"Don't turn your nose up at a silver – use it as a stepping-stone."

"It's not the medal," Ciara told him. "It's the time. Come on, Mark. Four fifty-nine?"

She shook her head with disappointment.

"Don't let it get you down, Ciara. That'll swamp you. Get angry instead. Turn your disappointment into something positive. Use it to your advantage."

"After all my training. I thought I was ready to win the 400 IM."

"You *are* ready. You're good enough to wipe the floor with any of them. It's nothing to do with your physical condition." He tapped his forehead. "It's all up here. It's all concentration. You need to buckle down to swimming and not get distracted. You've got to focus your thinking. I'll bet your thinking was all over the place in that race."

Ciara looked at him. He went on.

"Look at your pattern in the race. You used up a quarter of it trying to flatten a nobody in another lane. You let her distract you. You weren't thinking through the next 300 metres. Instead, you were thinking of beating someone in the second length. You'd no energy left to race the last part. You were struggling and completely burnt out. That's nothing to do with your fitness level and everything to do with your head."

Ciara picked up her kit-bag. She didn't feel able to analyse what had gone wrong right now. Maybe later. "I'm going to shower," she said to Mark.

She stood in the hot showers, her disappointment turning to anger as she realised that Mark's words were right. How could she have been so stupid?

120

She was a lot better than that. Her personal best was three seconds faster than she'd swum the race. She was fit. Her technique was good. It was her concentration that was the problem.

She thought back through the race. God, she'd even let her mind wander to comparing Susan's breaststroke with Sorcha's. During a race! She wouldn't expect the little kids of six and seven to be that naive, yet here she was looking at somebody's stroke technique during a major final. And she had burnt herself out in her rush to get past a novice in the second length. Her last length had been a struggle as a result. How could she be so stupid?

She combed out her hair and pulled on a clean sweatsuit, packing her wet gear into her kit-bag.

As she emerged from the changing rooms, the award ceremony was being announced. First, second and third of each event lined up in order for their medals. Ciara joined Susan and Rachel in the line-up and received her silver medal, her disappointment forgotten in the excitement and the cheers of her swimming friends.

Afterwards, she went up to the spectators gallery where the rest of the club's swimmers were sitting.

"Well done, Ciara," they called encouragingly.

"A good race!"

"Way to go, Ciara."

Ciara smiled her appreciation and showed them her medal. As nobody had a swim coming up for a while, a few of them decided to leave the spectator seating to grab a snack and a drink in the café. Ciara glanced down towards the pool area as they were filing out. Across in the swimmers' gallery, she caught sight of Mark noting times and forms on his clipboard. As she turned to follow the others, his words echoed in her brain.

"You've got to focus your thinking, Ciara. Concentrate. It's all in your head."

Chapter 10

Mary-Anne squinted across the playing-fields. The low March sunlight was bright white and made it difficult for her to see. She shielded her eyes from the glare. She could just make out the roof of the little games hut among the shrubbery on the far side of the field.

The playing-fields were deserted, games cancelled for the afternoon. There was frost covering the pitches. It had been bitterly cold the last few days. The playing-fields were on the north side of the school so that even the thin rays of the midday sun didn't manage to melt the ice that laced the grass.

"I bet that's where he went with her," Mary-Anne said. "We'll give him a scare by bursting in on them."

Mary-Anne had decided she needed to come down a bit heavier on Eoghan. Keep him in line. He was getting a bit too interested in Sorcha for Mary-Anne's comfort and she wanted to nip it in the bud.

"She's something else," he'd told Mary-Anne. "Wouldn't mind getting to know her a bit better."

"I know what your idea of 'getting to know someone' means!" Mary-Anne told him.

Mary-Anne reckoned that Sorcha wasn't Eoghan's type at all. A bit of a greenhorn when it came to guys. Not like Mary-Anne herself, who knew exactly what Eoghan liked; except that Eoghan himself hadn't noticed yet.

Then again, if you were someone who swam up and down a pool every free minute you had, you were hardly going to be up on all the tricks guys tried to pull. And you certainly needed to be up early in the morning to get the better of Eoghan – even earlier than Sorcha. He could be dead convincing. He was already putting on a big show for her: walking her to the pool in the evenings, offering to join her for lunch, even sitting with her in Mr Barrett's classes. And it was prickling Mary-Anne. She was feeling a little sour about it all. The next thing would be a bit of harmless larking around, canoodling. Some sweet talking to soften Sorcha up a bit. A kiss and cuddle, bit of a grope.

And wham! It would all go from there.

Chain reaction.

Mary-Anne would be out of the equation for good.

What Eoghan lacked in smoothness, he made up for in tenacity. Mary-Anne knew that, unless she sorted this out, he'd stick to Sorcha like a limpet until she started going out with him.

"I know what he's like, Katie," she turned to her. "This is all for Sorcha's protection, you realise? She's got it coming and I don't think she'd notice if it was a ten-ton truck. She hasn't a clue about Eoghan's intentions. Probably even thinks they're honourable!" Mary-Anne gave a loud laugh but Katie was distracted by other things.

"What if Miss Keenan catches us? We're supposed to be in the library," she whimpered from behind Mary-Anne.

"Don't get in a panic about that," Mary-Anne assured her. "Miss Keenan is so distracted by her latest boyfriend that she wouldn't notice if the whole class went missing. You know that yourself. You were the one with the news on that front."

Mary-Anne turned back and squinted across the fields again. "I bet they're in there. Where else would Eoghan go with Sorcha? The games hut, of course, where nobody's likely to be."

Katie smiled in admiration at Mary-Anne's powers of deduction.

"Come on, we're going to sneak up on them and give them the fright of their lives," Mary-Anne continued.

"Is that a good idea?" Katie asked. "It's probably none of our business what they're up to."

Mary-Anne looked at Katie in astonishment. She couldn't believe the stuff Katie came out with at times.

"Katie, what are you talking about?" She spoke slowly to her, pausing between each word to give it time to sink into Katie's soft-boiled brain. "Of course it's our business. Eoghan wants to do with Sorcha what he wants to do with every girl in the school. He wants to get past first base with her. Get his jollies. Bonk her. This is Eoghan we're talking about. *Comprenez?* The guy has a mind like a sewer, and Sorcha hasn't a clue. We need to watch out for her."

Mary-Anne turned from Katie and began crossing the field. The frozen grass crunched and squeaked as she walked across it. The ice crackled as Katie followed her hesitantly.

The games hut had no windows. It was a battered wooden structure where football nets and balls, spare hurls and *sliotars*, tennis racquets, rounders bats, athletics equipment and the odd lost trainer were stored. The door was held closed with a rusty bolt that was pad-locked at the end of the school day. As they approached it, the girls could see the door was slightly ajar, the bolt open.

"Right," Mary-Anne hissed. "Watch this for a good reaction."

She marched right over and yanked open the door.

She stood still and stared in, in silence.

Watching her from a short distance away, Katie waited for a moment. When nothing happened, she walked over and peered in also.

The hut was empty but for the usual heaps of equipment around the floor and against the walls. A half-dead bluebottle buzzed dozily around in the dusty air.

"Damn," muttered Mary-Anne, slamming the door closed, her brow furrowed.

"Do you think he heard us coming, then?" Katie enquired.

They were interrupted by a shout from the other side of the pitch.

"Get back here, you scoundrels," a voice cried.

"Oh, no," groaned Katie, turning towards the unwelcome sight of Mr Barrett skipping towards them across the frozen fields. "This is all we need."

He stopped when halfway across the field and called to them, his breath coming in steaming white clouds. "Katie and Mary-Anne, get over here now. Your persistent disobedience is intolerable."

Katie began walking glumly towards the school and the teacher. Mary-Anne ignored them both, staring with puzzlement at the games hut. Where had Eoghan and Sorcha got to?

Miss Keenan walked back down to the library after re-organising her classes for the next day. The weather in March was always so unpredictable. If it wasn't frost on the pitches, it was endless rain or sleet. It messed up her classes every year. At least she'd sorted out tomorrow and had booked the library for the day. She'd have to prepare some work on the rules of camogie and football, have some theoretical classes instead.

As she approached the library, she was alarmed to hear absolutely no noise from the class inside. Silence was always ominous when there was an entire class left unsupervised. Especially when it was this particular transition year, who tended to be noisier and wilder than most. Yells and clatters and shouts were reassuring; signs of life, a signal that everything was OK.

Something must have happened to cause this silence.

Quickening her step, she pulled open the heavy library door and almost walked into the back of Mr Barrett who was addressing the entire class in his dulcet tones.

". . . and the brazenness of some of you to abandon your designated room in favour of the games hut . . . "

He turned on hearing her come in and smiled, inclining his head slightly.

"Miss Keenan, I must apologise for interrupting your class, but I found two of your students out on the games pitch, scouting around the games hut. I know this transition year are a tedious lot and I avoid them as much as I can, but I felt obliged to address this issue with them all."

Miss Keenan smiled. Mr Barrett was a hoot with his little airs and graces and funny ways. You couldn't help but like him. He drove the kids scatty, but they had the height of respect for him and there was certainly never any misbehaviour in his classes. That explained the perfect silence.

"Thanks a million, Mr Barrett. I'm going to let them get on with some study for the rest of the session. Is everybody here now?"

She glanced over the rows of faces, making sure that the usual troublemakers were all present. Most of them sat in a bunch together, chewing gum or pencils. Yes, there were Mikey and Thomas, muttering to each other. Claire was behind them. And Katie and Mary-Anne, the two guilty culprits, were standing by the door, their faces red with embarrassment.

That was everyone. Or was it? Miss Keenan did another quick sweep of the room.

Eoghan was missing.

His six-foot frame was difficult to conceal. He normally stuck out like a sore thumb in every class and, if you didn't see him, you usually heard him.

He'd hardly have sneaked off on his own and, as Mary-Anne and Katie were here, who was he with? It took Miss Keenan a few moments to notice that Sorcha was missing also. Well, well, well. Who'd have thought the two of them would head off together? Off up to devilment somewhere, no doubt. She turned to Mr Barrett.

"Honestly, Mr Barrett. Would you credit it? I'm gone five minutes to arrange some class details and four people absent themselves from class without permission. Luckily, you've found two of them."

Turning back to the class, she raised her voice.

"What do you lot take me for? I can't leave you alone for any length of time but you all start messing. I can understand Mr Barrett's sentiments exactly when he says he has as little as possible to do with you."

"It wasn't all of us, miss," someone retorted. "I said nothing. I'm sitting here minding my own business since you left. It's not my fault."

This outburst received a murmur of support from some of the others.

Mr Barrett turned to her.

"Now, Miss Keenan," he said. "Why don't you remain here and supervise this miserable lot? I shall take myself off and locate those escapees. I have a free class now, so it's no trouble."

Miss Keenan took a deep breath.

"Thank you, Mr Barrett, but I'd much rather find them myself. I need to give them a good talking-to. Would you mind staying here instead?"

Mr Barrett raised his eyebrows. "If you're quite sure?"

Miss Keenan smiled. "I'm certain. Thank you. I shan't be any longer than necessary."

Pleased that the class were now to be properly supervised. Miss Keenan left the library to find Eoghan and Sorcha. Where would she begin? She'd hadn't gone far down the school corridor when somebody called her.

"Excuse me, Miss," Mary-Anne Darke closed the library door after her and ran up to Miss Keenan.

"Well, Mary-Anne?"

"Miss, me and Katie were looking for Sorcha and Eoghan too. Mr Barrett said to come after you and tell you that we've looked in the games hut but they're not there. Just to save you the trouble, like."

Miss Keenan nodded at her. "Thank you, Mary-Anne."

As Mary-Anne headed back to the library, Miss Keenan considered her options. Where could they have gone? There were the cloakrooms, the gym hall, the lunch-rooms. They may have left school altogether and headed off to the chipper or the snooker hall. She glanced at her watch. A bit early for that – they'd have to miss two other classes also. She made her way to the cloakrooms, knowing that Eoghan had hung out there before. Mind you, he'd also been caught so maybe once bitten, twice shy.

She passed the gym on the way and paused at the door. Surely not. The big gym was too exposed. Anyone popping in would see them immediately. Nowhere to hide. Still, no harm trying. Miss Keenan opened the door and looked. The hall was completely empty. Stepping in, her trainers squeaked on the polished wooden floor, the sound echoing round the walls. Glancing down at the spectator's gallery, Miss Keenan couldn't see anyone. She paused for a moment, looking again at the gallery. Beneath the slant of the seating plinths, there was a small storage area where the gymnastic mats and springboards were stacked. Smiling to herself, and not really believing that the two renegades had hidden in there, she walked across the floor to the low wooden door of the store. Grasping the wooden knob of the small door, she pulled and, bending over, peered in.

The store area was dark, lit only by the lights from the gym hall. Miss Keenan could see only the first three or four feet, but knew it was deep as it continued the length of the gallery. It smelled musty and rubbery from the well-used mats that were heaped on the floor. There was no immediate sign of anyone, but a small rustle betrayed their presence.

They were there all right.

Miss Keenan straightened up.

"Come out here, the two of you. Immediately."

Eoghan had been inclined to withdraw further into the darkness and not say anything. After all, Miss Keenan couldn't be sure it was them and she wasn't going to crawl in after them. Eoghan knew that it was worse for him with the sentence he had hanging over him, so he'd have preferred to hide. But the sharpness of Miss Keenan's voice had Sorcha scrambling out in an instant. She gave Eoghan a puck and had him crawl out first. He emerged on all fours, unable to fit through the doorway any other way. He squinted in the brightness as he stood up.

"Fix your clothes, young man," Miss Keenan instructed him icily.

Eoghan was mortified. He straightened his tie, tightening the knot, and quickly tucked in his shirt.

Sorcha followed immediately, creeping out from the dark storage area and straightening up, also squinting in the light. Her eyes were downcast, her face worried-looking. She stood in front of the teacher, without saying a word.

"What is the meaning of this?" Miss Keenan began.

Eoghan groaned to himself. His teacher's voice was soft and controlled. He hated it when they began like that. Give him fire and brimstone anytime. Bible-thumping and endless rattling on and on were a doddle to handle. He could cope with it a lot better when they stamped and yelled and shouted at him. But a teacher who was quiet and still was awful. And far more dangerous because it usually meant they were seething.

He glanced at Miss Keenan. True enough, she was a picture of simmering anger. Eoghan could see the tell-tale veins in her neck pulsing with anger. Like a snake about to bite.

"Oh, my God," Eoghan thought, "I'm a goner. That's me out on my ear for a two-week suspension." How could he be so stupid? He had managed to struggle through a few months with no black marks, which was a major achievement, only to collect about fifty in one go this time round.

"Eoghan wanted to talk to me, Miss," Sorcha volunteered.

Miss Keenan looked at her closely, not really believing her innocence, but Sorcha looked sincere.

"In the mat store? Oh come on, Sorcha. Why couldn't you just talk in the library?" Miss Keenan asked.

"It was private," Sorcha told her, glancing at Eoghan. "Eoghan needed to talk to me in private."

"Private. Well, Eoghan?" Miss Keenan turned to him expectantly. "Maybe you'd like to talk to me about your private matters?"

He went red under his teacher's gaze.

"Em . . . no, thanks, Miss," he muttered.

"Of course not. I don't want you to, either." Miss Keenan looked at him wearily. "Do you think I came down in the last shower, Eoghan?" she demanded at last.

She launched into a lecture on irresponsibility and recklessness and getting others into trouble. Sorcha was included and found herself upbraided for having got into such an unacceptable situation so early in her school year.

By the time Miss Keenan had run out of things to say, they were all a bit bedraggled and weary. She frogmarched them to Mrs Graham's office. Mrs Graham tutted a bit, but she could see they'd all had enough at that stage. So, instead, she decided that both Sorcha and Eoghan should return the next morning to be told their fate. Eoghan and Sorcha looked at each other sulkily from opposite sides of the office before being escorted back to the library.

Chapter 11

"What? Reduce my swimming sessions when we've bought a new house nearby so that I can increase my training? I don't believe what you're suggesting, Mark."

Ciara was incredulous. Here was Mark, proposing that she no longer come to the pool four mornings a week, but three mornings one week and one morning the next in a fortnightly pattern. This was her first morning back at training after the disappointment of the Silver Fish meet. Bringing home a silver medal from second place in the 400-metre Individual Medley had been less than she had hoped for. It certainly knocked her for six and made her realise that she needed to put in more training if she was to scoop a couple of gold medals in the Leinsters. So she had arrived this morning all fired up and ready to work hard on her training when Mark asked to speak with her and then landed this on her, totally unexpected.

"Calm down," Mark smiled at her. But that only incensed her further. Nothing infuriated her more when she was hassled about something than being told to calm down. Ciara frowned at him, tears of frustration and disappointment pricking her eyes. She tried to keep her voice steady.

"But you want me to reduce my practice times by almost five hours. I need to get better, Mark. I need to win some competitions. You're suggesting that I train for fewer hours. It doesn't seem to make any sense. The Silver Fish was a disaster. I can't believe how badly I did. I've only just got accustomed to the new routine and it's working, but I need more time at it to get ready for the Leinsters. You've seen how my race times have dropped. I've knocked several seconds off all my events. How will I manage to improve my times more if you get me to train less?"

"It's part of your new schedule," Mark continued, speaking softly and with authority. This decision was not open to negotiation and he wanted Ciara to understand that clearly. "The Silver Fish was not a disaster. It was your first major competition since starting on a new routine and you have to learn lessons from it. That's why I'm changing your routine now. Your times have dropped significantly," he acknowledged. "That's great, but you're not swimming your optimum during competitions, and that's the crucial part. You're several seconds outside your best in most competition events and you're being beaten by weaker swimmers. Yet you're in top physical shape and you're swimming impressive times in training. So there's some kind of problem there, right? I mentioned it to you at the Silver Fish meet, but it wasn't a good time to talk about it. But now it is. You're back at training and the next major competition is the Leinsters. We have to look at tackling this problem in time for them. There's no point in swimming up and down a pool endlessly when you're already at your peak. First of all, you'll get weary of the routine and lose interest. Nobody can sustain maximum motivation unless there's change and challenge."

Ciara leaned across and picked up her track suit top from where she had left it on the diving blocks. Standing on the poolside got a bit chilly after a few minutes and it looked like this might take longer than she had anticipated.

"Secondly," Mark went on, "what are you aiming for? Knocking seconds off your times is good – but not only during training sessions. We've got to get you to transfer your improved times to a competition, so that you're swimming your best *and* beating others. You need to be able to concentrate your mind and your body so that you're not distracted. Just a second."

He walked over to the poolside and told two of the other swimmers their next drill, demonstrating the leg kick he wanted them to work on. Ciara watched him. She felt gutted. His words were a real slap in the face for her. She'd thought endlessly about the Silver Fish since coming home and had figured that, if she trained for every possible minute between now and the Leinsters, she'd be ready to go for gold. She'd worked through her disappointment. Her dad had talked it over with her, reasoning out that she'd been through undue stress, what with changing schools and moving house, not to mention living with her gran. All the upheaval was bound to impact on her ability to concentrate. She'd come back to training now, ready to fight and win again, when Mark had hit her with this devastating news. He joined her again.

"Now, where was I?" he asked.

"You were saying that I need to concentrate. But I don't see how reducing my swimming hours can improve my concentration. Nor do I see how reducing my training is going to make a routine any more interesting. I'll just have less time to fit in the same drills, which will put me under greater pressure."

She put her head down so that Mark wouldn't see how really disappointed she was.

"Hey, hold on a second," Mark bent over and looked up at her face. "Don't look so dejected. I haven't finished yet. Just let me explain what I have in mind."

Ciara looked at him, not in the least convinced by his words. He continued.

"I agree with you. Reducing your hours won't improve your concentration, but I've organised for somebody to come in and help out with that. All the major swim clubs have coaches who come in and get the swimmers mentally ready for competitions. These people don't do pool or dry-land training, but they look at the mental attitudes of the swimmers and what distracts them before and during competitions. Then they try and work on a plan to reduce distractions and improve concentration during events. It goes hand in hand with physical training so that both programmes complement each other. It's a bit like my pep talk, but more structured and aimed at each swimmer's weak spots."

"Like the positive mental attitude stuff you go on about?" Ciara asked, her curiosity aroused. "It's sport psychology, am I right?" She'd heard about it at the galas and read about it in the swimming journals.

"Exactly. It's to get you psyched up and ready for an event," Mark replied. "It's something you need, Ciara. Not because you don't have a positive mental attitude, but because you've been through a lot of changes this year and they're bound to affect your performance in competition. This will give you some techniques to block out distractions and focus your mind."

Ciara shrugged. She had to admit to herself that it sounded reasonable. Her personal bests in all events were better that her competition times in the Silver Fish, so maybe this person could help sort that out. But she had a couple of questions to ask.

"So why do I have to reduce my training times for that?"

"Two reasons. First, this coach is going to work with the swimmers one morning a week during your usual training time, so you'll be missing swimming then, but you'll still be down here at her session. It'll be a group discussion followed by individual talks in the gym. And second, I want the other mornings to be sleep-ins for you. One of the attending doctors I was talking to at the Silver Fish meet explained about overuse of the muscles and how it can cause muscle fatigue. It's a serious problem with top international swimmers and athletes who suffer frequent injuries to muscles and ligaments from overuse. Strained ligaments and muscle weakness are common symptoms. Muscle fatigue will set in if you're working the same set of muscles without allowing recovery time and it seriously hinders progress. You're doing a massive amount of heavy training, possibly too much. We need to build in a bit of recovery time for your muscles to allow them to prepare for the next onslaught. That's why it'll be one week on, one week off, from now on. In that way, every second week your muscles get to rest in the mornings. I'm preparing a fitness maintenance programme for you."

"And what about my tedious routine that might make me lose motivation?" Ciara demanded, grinning slightly. "How are you tackling that one?"

Mark smiled slightly. "I've done a little creative re-arranging of your actual sessions. We'll be maintaining your levels of stamina and strength, but your actual sessions will have a minimum amount of continuous length swimming, and more variety."

Ciara curled her lip with immediate dislike. "It sounds like I'm going to be part of a swimming-pool variety club. Are you sure this is going to work? I mean, I'm not into synchronised swimming!"

"Ciara," Mark cried in mock disgust, "just give things a chance. When have I ever let you down?"

"No comment," replied Ciara, her spirits recovering somewhat now that Mark had gone through the reasons with her. It all sounded OK, if a bit disappointing; but if she tried it out until the Leinsters in May, only a few weeks away, surely it couldn't do any harm.

Once she got back into the pool and did a few warm-up lengths, Ciara felt herself relax . The water always did that to her. She could get in wound up with all kinds of hassles and worries and, after a few lengths, they'd all have melted away, dissolved in the water. It was working its old magic now. After a while, the reduction in her swimming hours didn't seem all that bad now that she realised Mark was still working very definitely towards a target of her winning some events in the Leinsters. Ciara had been worried that he was breaking it to her gently that she needed to review her future in swimming after her performance in the Silver Fish. But he didn't seem to think that it was such a big deal after all. If anything, he was quite upbeat about the whole thing, telling her what she could learn from it, and coming back with his new sports psychology ideas and information about muscle fatigue. If all his plans fell into place and if she stuck to the new programme, things might not work out so badly.

When she'd finished her training, she checked her schedule that week with Mark. He confirmed for her that she had the next morning off and no morning session until the following Friday. It felt odd knowing she could sleep in the next morning but she had to admit that the sound of it was appealing.

Back at home, her parents had already arrived round to Granny's place. Today they were moving into their new house. Her mum and dad had taken the day off work. Sorcha and Ciara were going to school as usual, but going round to their new home that evening. Ciara was excited about having her own room with all her bits and pieces around her again.

Her parents and granny were in the kitchen, chatting. Sorcha was at the table having breakfast.

"I'm starving," Ciara announced as she joined them. "Any chance of a couple of slices of bacon and toast?"

"What did your last slave die of?" her mother demanded jokingly as she placed two rashers on the grill and some bread in the toaster. She was dressed in working clothes for the move – jeans and sweatshirt, with her hair tied up under a headscarf. "How did the swimming go?"

"Fine," said Ciara, filling a bowl with cereal and slicing a banana on top. "Mark wants to reduce my morning training sessions to between one and three each week."

"About time he saw some sense," said Sorcha. "I keep telling everyone that the human system can't take early mornings, and does anyone listen to me? Mark probably had to wait until some bigwig scientist did a major study only to find out that what I've been saying all along is true."

Her father looked at Ciara. "Why didn't he do this before we all upped and left our old house? Could have saved me a fortune if he'd reduced your training sessions last year."

Ciara grinned at her father, knowing he was only teasing her. She explained Mark's plan as she demolished a sizeable breakfast and then ran upstairs to bring down her suitcase of clothes and boxes of books and belongings.

"Here, let me help you with those." Her father came into the hall as she slid a third box down the stair carpet. "You'd better go in and have a chat with your gran. She'd going to miss having the two of you around and she's feeling a bit lonely."

Granny was sitting on her own in the kitchen, having a cup of tea. Sorcha and her mum were loading cases and boxes into the back of the car through the front door.

"I'll drop round and see you after school tomorrow, Gran," Ciara began. "I'm only down the road from you now, so it'll be no problem getting here. Anyway, I'll have to pick up my bike because Dad doesn't think he can fit it in the car today."

"It'll be great for you getting to your swimming now, Ciara," Gran told her, ruffling Ciara's hair affectionately. "But I'll miss the pair of you round the house. It's been nice having company these last few weeks."

Ciara put her arms round the old woman. "Don't worry," she assured her. "We're like bad pennies – we're always turning up. You'll be sick of the sight of us!"

Granny smiled at her through pale eyes. "I'd never be sick of you, dear," she told her.

"Come on, Ciara," Sorcha called from the hall. "We'll be late for school. It's already ten to nine."

Ciara gave her gran a sound kiss and a hug, promising she'd drop over the following day, before grabbing her schoolbag and heading out the door. Her parents were tying down the lid of the boot.

"This is getting to be a habit," their dad said.

"We'll see you girls at the new house after school. Try to get home as soon as possible so you can sort your rooms out," their mother smiled at them.

They were almost at the school gates before Sorcha told Ciara that she had to go to the principal's office that morning.

"Why?" Ciara asked.

"Because I spent some time with Eoghan yesterday," Sorcha told her.

"There's nothing wrong with that," Ciara replied.

"We were hiding in a store cupboard together."

"What? I don't believe it, Sorcha," Ciara stopped dead in her tracks. "When?" She opened the door of the school and they walked down the corridor leading to the cloakroom.

"It was during class-time."

"Oh, Sorcha," Ciara looked with dismay at her sister. "What happened?"

Sorcha groaned. "My God, talk about getting the third degree! I don't know if I even wanted anything to happen. But that was yesterday. Now I feel different about it all. Eoghan has being going on and on about how much he likes me and that we should be spending more time together. I mean, he's nice and stuff, but I thought he was a bit of a headcase. Anyway, when games were cancelled, he asked me to go for a walk with him . . ."

Ciara raised her eyebrows. "A walk! What exactly is that supposed to mean?"

Sorcha threw her eyes up to heaven and continued. "We ended up in the gym hall and then he decided we were too obvious. You know, just . . . there in the middle of the hall like two goldfish in a bowl if anyone decided to look in. So he suggested we crawl into the store cupboard."

"Don't tell me you fell for that one!" For somebody who was so together, Sorcha could be really stupid at times.

"You would have done the same!" Sorcha retorted hotly.

"Go on," Ciara encouraged her. They were in the cloakroom now, hanging up their coats.

"We started kissing," Sorcha lowered her eyes, her face getting pink. Ciara stood, waiting. "And then we got into some more stuff . . ."

This was more than Ciara expected. "What kind of 'stuff', Sorcha? How far did you go?"

Sorcha looked at her sharply. "We didn't go the full way, if that's what you want to know." She paused before continuing. "It was fun, but we were caught by Miss Keenan."

"Are you saying you would have gone the whole shebang with him? Only that the teacher arrived?"

Sorcha busied herself with adjusting the strap on her schoolbag. "Maybe," she muttered.

"What?" Ciara stared at her. "Sorcha, you've just said this guy is a headcase. But you're telling me that if Miss Keenan hadn't arrived, you'd have shagged him?"

"I told you I thought he was a headcase. But he's not. People don't understand him, that's all. He's funny. And he thinks I'm great. He makes me feel good."

Ciara shook her head as she sat down on the bench. "Was he planning all this? I mean, did he have . . . protection with him?"

Sorcha grabbed her bag and swung it over her shoulder. "Don't be so bloody ridiculous. I knew I shouldn't have talked to you about it," she burst out. "I might have guessed you wouldn't understand anything!"

With that, she stormed out of the cloakroom, leaving Ciara sitting on the bench staring after her.

Chapter 12

"What am I supposed to do with myself for two weeks? Sit at home and twiddle my thumbs?" Eoghan demanded.

"You could catch up on all the old episodes of the soaps," Katie suggested. "*Sky 1* is showing them in the mornings. I'd love it."

Eoghan gave her a withering look. They were in their usual haunt in the cloakroom during the morning coffee break. Eoghan had just returned from a gruelling session in Mrs Graham's office. His face was still burning from the discomfort. Sorcha had been there too but she had got off lightly, being new to the school and it being her first misdemeanour. She still looked pretty shook however and, at one stage, Eoghan thought she was going to start crying. But she held it in, with just her lower lip quivering while she stared at the carpet the whole time. Mrs Graham had advised her to stay away from the likes of Eoghan and to choose her friends with greater care.

Eoghan was disgusted.

She didn't have to say that kind of stuff in front of him. She could have had the decency to say it in private to Sorcha, but no, Mrs Graham dragged it all out while he was sitting there. Sorcha had been given detention and dismissed. She hadn't even glanced towards Eoghan on her way out. That kind of stung him.

Then it was his turn.

"Did she really make you squirm?" Mary-Anne wanted to know now, her eyes shining.

"You're getting a real kick out of this, aren't you?" Eoghan said. "You're a sadist."

"Oooh, that's a big word!" Mary-Anne teased him.

"Do your parents know?" Katie wondered. That was her one fear.

"Of course they bloody well know," Eoghan's temper flared as he recalled Mrs Graham's phone call to his mother. She had hit the roof when she'd heard he'd been suspended for two weeks. Eoghan could hear her shriek over the phone from where he sat at the other side of the office. Even Mrs Graham had winced. He'd be skinned tonight, for sure.

"I'd love a fortnight off this place," Mary-Anne said with great sincerity. "It'll be great, Eoghan. You can sleep late in the mornings, and doss round the house all day."

Eoghan looked at her. "It's all right for you to say," he said miserably. "Mrs Graham still wants me to sit the Easter exams *and* I have to pass everything or else she's going to throw me out of school. That means I have to work my butt off at home. She said she's sick of the time and effort she's put into me and my family. Me and my family! I can't take the blame for my older brothers. I've nothing to do with their carry-on."

He also had two younger brothers coming up behind him in the school.

"And she says she has another seven years of my family to put up with. She said she may take early retirement."

Mary-Anne laughed at the thought of Mrs Graham taking early retirement because of Eoghan's family. They were interrupted by the bell announcing the end of coffee break.

"Right, I'm off," Eoghan announced. "I'm not hanging round here any longer than necessary." He pulled a letter from Mrs Graham out of his pocket. "I've to bring this home to my mam who's waiting for me in the house."

"Oh, Eoghan!" Mary-Anne cried, feigning wails of sorrow and grabbing him in a bear hug. "Give me a big kiss."

"Leave me alone," Eoghan told her, pushing her away. "Buzz off."

"Will we see you in the snooker hall later on?" she asked him.

"I doubt it," Eoghan told her. "I'm probably grounded until my old age pension comes through."

"Good luck," Katie called as she went off to class.

"I'll give you a ring," Mary-Ann promised.

"Sure," Eoghan replied, standing watching them as

they disappeared round the corner. Once he was on his own, he sank down on the bench again, dejected. This was no joke. His dad was going to hit the roof when he heard.

Eoghan decided not to go straight home. He couldn't face the thought of his mother, who would be all wound up and ready to let fly at him. She'd have just got it all out of her system and he'd have to face it all again when his father got in from work. The thought of it was killing him. The longer he put it off, the better. He wanted to get out of the school, but heading straight home didn't sound too appealing. He decided to mosey round to the snooker hall for an hour or so, just to loosen up. Cool off a bit.

Sorcha on the other hand had recovered quickly from her ordeal, mainly because she was so furious at Ciara's Miss Goody-two-shoes reaction that Mrs Graham's lecture had merely been a distraction. She'd been given detention and the usual warnings about watching herself and not mitching, but that was about it. She had been somewhat uncomfortable in the office, especially with Eoghan sitting there listening while she was warned about the folly of hanging round with him, but as soon as she got outside and spent a bit of time thinking about it, she reasoned that she'd done OK.

In the first class after coffee break, Mary-Anne and Katie came up to her.

"How did you get on?" Mary-Anne asked.

"OK, I think. Mrs Graham wasn't too rough on me. I've got detention, but I expected that."

Mary-Anne nodded. Then she went on, "You know Eoghan's been chucked out?"

Sorcha was astounded. "What? Because of yesterday?"

Katie snorted.

Mary-Anne explained. "Not quite. He's had it hanging over him for a couple of months now. You were the final straw."

"That's terrible. What'll he do now?"

"Catch up on the soaps, I expect," Katie said.

"What?" Sorcha looked at her, confused.

"Don't mind her," Mary-Anne replied. "He's not gone for good. Two-week suspension, so he'll be back in time for the exams."

"Is he really upset?" Sorcha asked.

"About being back in time for the exams? He's not too pushed on that one, I suppose, but he's not been given a choice," Mary-Anne said.

"No, I mean about being suspended," Sorcha would have died if she'd been suspended for two weeks. What would her parents say?

"I think he's a bit hassled about it," Katie told her. "His dad will go ape when he finds out."

"I'll bet."

"I don't think Eoghan's going to be rushing home to his mammy's arms today."

"Is he still in the school?"

"No. Ran like a scalded cat as soon as the bell went."

151

Sorcha thought about Eoghan a lot during class that morning. Suspension. That was really tough. Something like that would have freaked her out.

Coming up to lunch-time, she wondered whether he was home yet and what his mother's reaction would be? She considered what Katie had said – that he wouldn't be rushing home. Where would she have gone if she needed time to think before heading home to face the music? It didn't take her long to decide. The snooker hall was the most likely place. It opened at half past eleven. Nobody was going to disturb you there and it was quiet at this time of day. Sorcha looked at her watch. Twelve-fifteen. If she scooted out of the school as soon as the bell went at lunch-time, she'd get round to the snooker hall and still be back in time for class that afternoon. It'd give her a chance to see Eoghan for a few minutes. After all, they were kind of in this together.

On the bell, Sorcha left class immediately without saying a word to Mary-Anne or Katie. The less attention she attracted to herself, the better. She grabbed her coat from the cloakroom and off she went, running down the street to the snooker hall. At the door of the hall, she paused for a moment.

What if he wasn't here?

What was she going to say if he was?

What was she even doing here?

She took a deep breath and pushed the door open.

The inside of the hall was gloomy compared to the

brightness outside. It took Sorcha's eyes a few moments to adjust to the dimness. The hall smelt awful – the stink of stale cigarettes hung in the air. She'd never noticed it before, but it really hit her now.

At first, Sorcha thought there was nobody at all there. The spectator gallery was empty. The snooker tables were in darkness.

But from the rows of one-armed bandits came the familiar sound of jangles and rattles and money clinking into slots. Sorcha could see a couple of people walking round the machines, feeding in coins and pulling the levers. With no great difficulty, she spotted Eoghan's head over the top of one of the one-armed bandits, his eyes down. She walked over.

"Hi, Eoghan."

He jerked his head up, clearly surprised. A big grin spread across his face when he saw who it was. "Sorcha! What are you doing here?"

He walked round to where she stood and put his hands on her shoulders.

"I just wanted to see if you were OK," she said, hugging him round the waist. "After this morning."

He shrugged, shaking a lock of hair out of his eyes. "I suppose I'll survive. I've the memory of you in the store cupboard to comfort me while I'm grounded."

Sorcha laughed. "Two weeks, huh? What a sentence."

He nodded in agreement. "A real bummer. The old man will freak." Then he asked, "You staying down here for a while? Keeping the condemned man company and all that."

Sorcha glanced at her watch. It was twelve-fifty. "Not quite. I've about twenty minutes. I've to be back for Mr Barrett's class at half past one."

"You wouldn't want to miss him, now would you?" Eoghan chuckled.

"Won't be the same without you beside me, trying to knock his eye out."

"Come on, I'll have time to beat you in a game of pinball before you head back."

Sorcha joined him and they started into the machines with gusto. Eoghan seemed to have no end of loose change in his pocket.

"Where do you get all this money?" Sorcha asked him as he fed coins into the slots.

"I win it," he told her. "The machines cough up about every twentieth game. So if you watch them carefully, you can guess which ones are about ready to spit. Never go near a bandit where someone's just won a load of money, because you can be sure you certainly won't."

"You'd have to be in here most of the time to get to know them." Sorcha couldn't think how anyone could spend so much time watching slot machines.

"You get to know them pretty quick," Eoghan assured her. "Here, try this one over here. It's just about ready to spew."

Sorcha followed him. True enough, after a couple of

tries, she hit the jackpot and a waterfall of twenty-pence pieces showered into the metal tray of the machine. Sorcha shrieked with delight. Eoghan laughed and they kissed in celebration of her win. They moved away from the slot machines after a while and tried out a virtual reality downhill slalom game.

"I've never done this before," Sorcha laughed as Eoghan got her to stand up on two mounted skis in front of a large screen that curved around her. "It's really scary."

The skis wobbled beneath her, swivelling around on brackets. She grabbed for him, steadying herself.

"Grab these," Eoghan told her. He put two ski poles in her hands. They, too, were attached to brackets and cables that fed into the whole contraption.

"OK, are you ready?" Without giving her time to answer, Eoghan pushed some change into the slot and programmed the race.

Standing awkwardly on the mounted skis, the screen in front of her now depicting a steep snowy hillside complete with red and yellow flags, Sorcha grabbed the ski poles and felt herself slithering out of control as the screen image pitched her forwards down the mountainside and into a race. On-screen skiers appeared on the left and right, and she twisted and turned, attempting to weave through the flags and avoid the other skiers. Sound effects surrounded her with the swish of skis on snow and the shouts of an imaginary crowd. She managed to keep her balance round the first corner and was catching up with the leader coming to the second bend. The wind whistled as she clipped the edge of a flag on her left and there was a sudden shriek as she realised that she had knocked some poor virtual skier off the edge of a cliff. Sorcha twisted away from the cliff edge in fright and lost her balance. While Eoghan grabbed her round the waist and held her up, the screen showed what would have happened if she had really been on skis. The image tumbled forwards and pitched her headlong into the snow where she rolled over the edge of the cliff and into an deep abyss. All this was accompanied by the screams of a shocked virtual crowd and the image of her two ski poles falling ahead of her.

Then the screen went black.

"You're dead," Eoghan told her matter-of-factly. "You threw yourself over a cliff."

Sorcha's heart was pumping. "That was so frightening! My stomach still feels like I'm falling." She clambered down from the skis. "Here, you try it. See if you can do any better."

Eoghan needed no encouragement to climb up. Sorcha fed in the money and he was off, ploughing past the flags and overtaking other skiers. What he lacked in style, he made up for with sheer recklessness. Several other skiers met with a sticky end as Eoghan careered through them, sending them into deep abysses.

"Hey. You've done this before," she cried as Eoghan

skidded round a corner and overtook the leader. Only when his on-screen image crashed through the final barrier with a shower of snow and a clatter of skis did Eoghan ease up.

"You're not the only sporty person round here," he said modestly.

"I don't think you should take up skiing full-time," Sorcha laughed as they left that game and looked round to see what else there was.

"I'm starving," Sorcha suddenly announced. "What time is it?"

She peered at her watch.

"Oh, my God!"

"What is it?" Eoghan asked her.

Sorcha looked up at him, her face pale with fright.

"It's quarter past two!" she whispered. "I've been here for almost an hour and a half. I've missed Fat Bat's class. I'm really in hot water now!"

Eoghan blinked at her. "What do you want to do?"

Sorcha was dumbfounded. "I don't know. I suppose I'll have to get back, but I'm going to get into terrible trouble."

"Snap!" said Eoghan glumly. "Join the club."

"I have to go," Sorcha made her decision. "Trouble or not, it'd only be worse if I stayed out longer. I really didn't mean to – my bag and everything is still at school. I'll have to get back there."

"At least say a proper good-bye to me before I face the firing squad," Eoghan said.

"Poor Eoghan," Sorcha muttered, suddenly realising that she'd miss him a lot while he was grounded. "Ring me and let me know when you'll be allowed out again." She smiled at him. "I'll have to organise a special celebration night for your release."

Chapter 13

"Isn't this great?" Ciara called out to Sorcha as they pedalled down the hill from their new house to the swimming-pool. "It's so easy to get to swimming."

Sorcha pumped the pedals to catch up with her sister. The early April sunshine was smudging the clouds pink and gold as they cruised in the gates of the pool and hopped off their bicycles. Opening the pool door, Sorcha wheeled her bike into the lobby, followed by Ciara, and they locked them together in the store area. Martha looked out from where she was working in the cupboard where the filter system was. She was measuring the chlorine levels in the pool water.

"Morning, girls. Isn't it a beautiful morning? I think spring has finally arrived."

"It's lovely," Sorcha agreed. They made their way to the changing rooms. "On the bank and it's only five-fifteen. I think I've beaten my own record," she said as they emerged from the changing rooms two minutes later.

"It's so easy when you only have to roll down the

hill," Ciara said. "And on a sunny morning, getting up is a doddle."

There were a couple of others already in the pool as they began their warm-up. The cool, clean water felt good as Sorcha launched herself into a relaxed one-hundred-metre front crawl. Ciara powered past her, sprinting up the pool in a stylish butterfly. Over the next few minutes, more swimmers arrived, as did Mark and one or two coaches. The programme was chalked up on the board, the floats and diving blocks sorted. The morning's training began in earnest.

During his pep talk, Mark spoke to them about the Leinsters. "We have five weeks left," he said. "Those of you who are attending the lectures in the mornings to get you ready for the race, there'll be two extra sessions, each week. So no swimming on Wednesdays."

"How are you feeling about the Leinsters?" Sorcha whispered to Ciara.

Ciara shrugged. "OK, I suppose. But then I was feeling OK about the Silver Fish and I was much slower than my best time. Having said that, this psychologist who's coming in to talk to us is great. She really makes it clear and she's been teaching us some stuff about concentration and stopping your mind from wandering all over the place."

"I'm glad I'm not in the gala," Sorcha went on as Mark spoke to individual swimmers about their training schedules coming up to the competition. "For one, my training has been so bad lately. I've got so out of shape that I'm really tired after school even without a morning swim. I'd be a hospital case if I tried a gala right now. And secondly, I'd have to travel down the night before. That's a Friday. And Friday night is my night out with Eoghan. I'm not missing that."

Ciara smiled. Sorcha was really smitten with Eoghan these days. Ever since he had been suspended, she thought he was the best thing since sliced bread. Ciara couldn't understand why that was such a great thing, but what did she know? Sorcha was always telling her that swimming was the only thing she knew anything about.

"He's great, Ciara. He's so strong, you know? It takes real guts to come out smiling after being suspended from school for two weeks and being grounded at home for three weeks. This Friday is his first night out in ages." Sorcha said as she sprawled across the bed in Ciara's room. "He's so gorgeous. And he's working really hard in class now that he's back at school, so there's no trouble any more."

Ciara didn't really feel it was her place to point out that although Eoghan might be trying his best, Sorcha herself was still in trouble at home for having got detention two weeks in a row for mitching from classes. Their parents weren't a bit happy that she was head over heels about him.

"He's a waster, Sorcha," her mother told her.

Sorcha didn't seem to care.

"I don't know what you see in him," Ciara told her. "He's a total loser. And I wouldn't trust him as far as I could throw him."

Ciara's attitude drove Sorcha scatty. She was so strait-laced and boring about it all.

"You wouldn't understand," Sorcha told her dismissively. "These things just go right over your head, Ciara. For a start, he's got this amazing knack with slot machines. They just *pour* out money whenever he plays them."

Ciara looked at her sister in amazement. "I can't believe you're big into somebody because they're good at playing *slot machines*!"

Sorcha smiled broadly like a cat who'd got the cream and hugged herself with delight. "That's not the best part, Ciara," she said emphatically. "He's such a stud! A great kisser. Really hot and steamy. And not just kissing. You know what I mean. . . ?" she trailed off, smiling wickedly at her sister. Ciara reacted just as Sorcha knew she would.

Ciara looked at her. "You're going to end up in trouble. Make sure he doesn't lead you up the garden path only to dump you, that's all," she told her.

"Right, into lanes please. Up on the blocks, front crawl sprint relays. In fifties. Are you ready?" Mark blew his whistle sharply and everybody on the poolside hopped up and sorted themselves into lanes. At the pip of the whistle, the first swimmer in each lane dived in and swam two lengths of the pool, racing the others. The next swimmer was poised on the block ready to dive in as soon as their team-mate touched the wall. The real trick was for the second swimmer to have already swung into the dive but still have their toes touching the diving block at the moment the incoming swimmer reached the wall. As a technique, it saved valuable time during a race, but the snag was trying to avoid launching off the diving block before the incoming swimmer touched. That would get the whole team disqualified.

"Sorcha, front crawl only," Mark shouted as Sorcha surfaced from her dive and started into breaststroke. "We're not doing Individual Medley. Listen!"

Some of the swimmers on the bank laughed as Sorcha waved her hand in apology.

"So, this being his first night on the razzle since being grounded, what special treats have you in store for Romeo?" Ciara asked as they cycled home after their training.

"Oh, Ciara," Sorcha said and she speeded up her pedalling. "I wouldn't want to upset you with too many juicy details, now would I? Let's just say I have a great night planned," she called over her shoulder as she whizzed past her sister.

Eoghan spent ages getting ready to go out that evening. He'd given himself a good scrub in the shower and an extra shave. Not that he needed to.

"Bum-fluff is all that grows on your face," his older brother teased him.

But he shaved again, anyway. Just in case. He wanted to keep his skin smooth – beard-rash was a real passion-killer. Nothing worse than giving a girl itchy blotches on her face.

He had a new dance album playing loudly on his sound system to liven himself up. Nothing like a bit of music to put him in the mood for a night out. Especially as it was his first night out in three weeks. It felt like forever since he'd been out on the town. The music thumped and crashed all over the house until his father banged on the ceiling downstairs with the handle of a broom.

"Turn that racket down!" he yelled up at Eoghan. "I can't hear myself think."

Eoghan grumbled as he lowered the music by a fraction. But, yes, overall he had to admit to himself, things were looking up. His suspension from school was over. His father was speaking to him again. And he was looking forward to a good night. He was calling round to Mary-Anne's first for pizzas and a couple of beers, and then on to the snooker hall for a few games. And, finally, out partying till late.

On with his jeans and his Docs. Opening his wardrobe, he scrutinised his selection of shirts. He pulled out a couple and examined them critically. White one? No, too nerdy. Maybe the denim? But there was a stain on the front of that. He examined the stain, sniffing it. Curry sauce. He'd have to get out of the habit of curry sauce on his chips. The only other clean shirt in the wardrobe was a grey flannel one he'd got from his gran last Christmas. That kind of shirt only impressed grannies. So it got put back.

The only thing for it was a raid on his older brothers' bedroom. They usually had a reasonable selection of clean shirts and they'd never miss one. He crept across the landing and opened the bedroom door. Switching on the light, he began going through the shirts in the cupboards.

Plenty of white.

And a good few blue ones.

A pink one! Yeuch, no thanks.

At the end of the rail, Eoghan glimpsed a bright, lime green shirt. He took it out and checked it over. It looked brand-new: still had the little pins holding a piece of cardboard under the collar.

"Nice shirt," he said, as the bright fabric picked up the light. "You'll do."

On his way out of the bedroom, he spotted a bottle of aftershave sitting on the dressing table. No harm in a splash. He unscrewed the top and poured a generous amount into his open palm. Rubbing his hands together, he patted his face with it. Then he rubbed the rest over his bony chest.

It took a second or two before the liquid began to sting his open pores, but sting it did. Eoghan's face suddenly felt as if it was on fire.

He yelped and hopped round the place, trying to rub some of the quickly evaporating stuff from his raw face but to no avail. Eoghan jumped up and down, trying to distract himself.

The door downstairs was torn open and his father roared up the stairs.

"Eoghan, turn the blasted music down and stop dancing round the place. The ceiling will fall in."

"Sorry, Dad."

Eoghan quickly turned off the light in his brother's room and scuttled back into his own bedroom to finish getting ready. The new shirt fitted him perfectly. He opened the top button and stood proudly in front of the mirror. Yes, he was satisfied. Grabbing his jacket, he headed downstairs, careful to button it up lest either of his brother catch a glimpse of the lime green.

"I'm off," he announced, sticking his head in the door.

"Phew! What a stink," his younger brother said as a cloud of aftershave drifted into the room in Eoghan's wake. "Everyone will smell you coming!"

"Don't mind him, Eoghan," his mother said. "Have a good evening."

"And behave yourself," his father added.

"Hey, Eoghan," his older brother called from the sofa. "I hope you haven't been in my room nicking after-shave. That smell's very familiar."

"I wouldn't touch your stuff," Eoghan replied, beating a hasty exit while the going was good.

He walked round to Mary-Anne's house and rang the bell. He could hear music blasting out from inside, so he rang the bell again, leaving his finger on it for a few seconds. Mary-Anne answered it almost immediately.

"Hang on, hang on, I'm coming," she said. "Phew, what a stink, Eoghan. You can't come in smelling like that! It'll all have to be fumigated tomorrow."

Eoghan pushed past her into the house. "Buzz off, Mary-Anne," he told her, opening up his jacket and taking it off. There was a shriek of laughter from behind him.

"Eoghan, look at your shirt! You're like a walking traffic beacon! Does it glow in the dark?" She switched off the hall light to check him out and then shouted to the others in the sitting-room. "Hey, Katie and Sorcha, come and see this. A giant glow-worm smelling like a bunch of flowers has just crawled into the hall."

Sorcha and Katie emerged from the kitchen where they were grating cheese on to pizzas. Katie burst out laughing, while Sorcha looked at Eoghan and smiled.

"I think you look great," she told him, slipping her arms round his waist and giving him a kiss.

Chapter 14

Ciara sat quietly on the wall outside the leisure centre in Athlone. The sun was warm on her back. She could feel the heat of it through her sweatshirt. It was a good feeling. She had been there for several minutes now, on her own, having given herself a full half-hour before she had to go inside to get ready for her race.

At first, she had been distracted by different activities going on around her. A group of kids on their way to play in a football match had walked by, dressed in black-and-white kits. Cars drove past. A little dog had scampered up to say hello.

She had also been distracted by the fact that her family hadn't yet arrived at the leisure centre to watch her race in the 400-metre Individual Medley finals at the Leinster championships. She had arrived down the previous day in the bus with the rest of the swimming club. Fourteen of the swimmers, with Mark and another swimming coach, had come down that bit early to prepare for the gala. Ciara had swum her heat that morning, qualifying well with seconds to spare.

Now the final was imminent.

It was her first final since she had swum the same event in the Silver Fish meet. It was important to her. She wanted her family to be there. To support her. To cheer for her. But her parents and Sorcha hadn't arrived.

What had happened?

They were planning to drive down that morning, leaving their home at half past ten. Ciara looked at her watch. Two-twenty now. It was a drive of about two hours, so they should have been here before lunch.

Ciara had only twenty minutes to go before changing into her swimming gear. She couldn't afford to let it bother her any more. She had an important race to swim; she had to block out her concerns, prepare herself for her event, with or without her family.

Ciara collected her thoughts and focused on her swimming and the final that she faced. Breathing deeply and slowly the way the sports psychologist had taught her, she narrowed her thoughts down so that the only thing on her mind was the 400-metre final.

She was no longer aware of people walking past.

Or voices from the park across the road.

Or her worries crowding in on her.

She thought through every stroke of the 400-metre Individual Medley. She pictured herself standing up on the diving block, in lane 5, curling her toes round the block, staring down at the clear, blue water. She imagined the whistle blowing and her, launching herself towards the water.

She went over the entire race in her mind's eye. The

pace of her lengths. The pool at Athlone was 25 metres, not 50 like in the Silver Fish. That meant 16 lengths for her race. The butterfly stroke was the first quarter. She would take that steadily, smoothly. She had to control herself and not put too much into it. Hold back on the huge surge she always felt at the opening stages. The first stroke, the first length. The pace of the race was set in that leading distance, testing her ability to tighten up her thinking and use it to her advantage, to settle into the rhythm and speed of the race.

After that came the backstroke. Her weakest of the four. A good place for a weak stroke, though. Second. She'd still have plenty of energy. Pace the others. Stay calm, steady. Try to keep down the choppiness that always slowed up her backstroke. Don't scoop too deeply on the pull-down or she'd lose precious distance by dipping up and down. If she could force herself to keep a steady pace for the back crawl, and hold her own, she'd do OK for the next stroke.

Moving into breaststroke at 300 metres. Third quarter. Her favourite leg of the race. Smooth and rhythmic, it was a sleek stroke, echoing natural movement in the water. She could slice through the water well on breaststroke and she'd now be starting to gather her resources to move up her position. Maybe get into third, or even second place, by the end of the breaststroke, giving her time to move up further in the front crawl during the last 100.

The last stroke – front crawl. Ciara's second good stroke. A relaxed crawler, she knew she'd be doing well if things had gone according to plan up to this. Her crawl would power her through the water. She could see herself moving steadily past the lead swimmer into the front of the pack. Leading the field from midway through the front crawl. She'd have to establish her place by the start of the final fifty. That would put her under pressure as she'd need to maintain it for two lengths while the others pulled out all the stops and charged to overtake. The other option was to hold back until the last twenty-five, but securing first place and holding firm seemed a softer option than slipstreaming in second and attempting to overtake in the last length. Too chancy. Last fifty – nail your colours to the mast. Grasp first position and hold on for dear life.

"Ciara."

Once she held her place and kept up a steady pace, things should be fine, even if it was a fast race . . .

"Ciara."

Damn. Who was interrupting her mental preparation?

"What is it?" Ciara turned towards the sound of the voice, her face a scowl of annoyance.

"Hey, don't bite." Mark held his hands up defensively. "I wanted to see how you were doing." He walked across the path to where Ciara sat on the wall. He peered at her closely. "Are you all right?"

"I'm fine. I'm getting myself ready for my race."

Mark looked at his watch. "You've a few minutes yet to go. No sign of your parents or Sorcha?"

"No."

Ciara stood up and stretched. She really wasn't in the mood for talking. She was so close to being ready. Completely paced and planned. She didn't want to push herself off balance or lose her focus by chatting to Mark about her family's whereabouts. She knew that he was trying to buoy her up, soothe her before the race, but Ciara didn't feel the need to be soothed.

She felt cool about this whole race.

Ice-cool.

"I'm not even nervous," she told Mark. "I'm so calm I'm frightening myself. I'm so hardened and honed for this race I feel like polished steel."

Mark looked at her strangely. "I know it was all my idea, but what has that psychologist has been telling you – polished steel!?"

Ciara looked at him, then turned to walk away.

"No offence, Mark, but I think I'd be better on my own right now."

Mark stood up, not sure how to respond. Ciara was always brittle before a race, but she usually behaved differently. Normally, she'd be dying to talk, talk, talk about anything just to take her mind off the race. To distract herself.

But not this time . . .

This time, Ciara seemed to know exactly what was happening and she was very much in control.

"I'll see you on the poolside in a few minutes, so," Mark said as he headed back to the centre.

At two-forty, Ciara returned to the changing rooms and put on her swimsuit and cap. She adjusted her goggles and snapped the elastic around her head before pulling on a sweatshirt and her pool shoes. She emerged from the changing rooms a few moments later to do a few stretches and a little limbering up on the poolside. The previous race was still being swum – the senior boys 400 IM – so Ciara sat on one of the poolside chairs to wait.

Looking up at the spectators sitting in the viewing gallery, she spotted Sorcha and her parents, sitting quietly watching the race. Ciara did a double-take. She couldn't believe her eyes. How long had they been there? How come they hadn't told her they'd arrived? She jumped up and ran up to them immediately.

"Hi! When did you arrive?" she asked as she reached her parents' seats. Sorcha was sitting a row ahead of them.

"We've just got here," her father replied. He looked tired and strained. Sorcha kept watching the race and didn't turn around.

"Why didn't you come and find me? I didn't know where you were. What happened?" Ciara said.

Her mother smiled at her, but it was a strange smile. Too wide. The kind of smile you plaster on when you're having your photo taken but you don't feel very smiley. Sort of put-on and forced-looking.

"We didn't want to distract you," she told Ciara.

Ciara sensed there was a problem. Maybe they'd had an argument in the car on the way down.

"Is everything all right?" she asked, looking closely at her mother and glancing over at Sorcha who was still watching the race intently. Ciara guessed they'd had a quarrel about Sorcha's lack of interest in competitive swimming, judging by her sister's silence and her feigned interest in the activities in the pool. Her parents had started getting on to her about it when Sorcha announced she wasn't swimming in the Leinsters. "Everything's fine, love." Her mother was a hopeless liar. "Go ahead and get ready for your race. We'll see you afterwards."

Ciara paused, wondering whether or not to ask further. She decided not to and was about to leave when Sorcha spoke unexpectedly.

"You may as well tell her," she stated flatly. "She knows something's up."

Ciara stared at Sorcha in surprise. Her parents stared at Sorcha too, but their expressions betrayed very different emotions. They both looked ready to explode.

"Well, that's lovely, Sorcha!" her mother started. "We've already been over this. We agreed not to tell Ciara anything until after her race. It's not fair on her. But you couldn't go along with that, could you?"

Sorcha said nothing.

Her father went on. "That's typical of you, Sorcha. You can never think of anybody but yourself. Always trying for sensational effect. The dramatics! The melodrama! Every time, without fail."

"What *is* going on?" Ciara demanded, looking from one to the other. "Will one of you tell me what the problem is?"

"I'm pregnant," Sorcha announced.

174

Ciara blinked and stared. She couldn't take her eyes off Sorcha.

Her mother sniffed and reached into her handbag for a tissue, which she pressed against her nose.

Her father ran his hands through his hair and cleared his throat.

Nobody moved after that. Ciara felt as if somebody had arrived with a huge blast-freezer and frozen her family into a mini *tableau*, while normal activity went on all around. They remained still and silent, their body language saying volumes, while people came and left their seats around them. There was the noise of swimmers churning through the turbulent water of the pool. There was a swell of cheering as the race being swum reached its climactic end. But none of the Vaughans moved.

Ciara was the first to crack the ice.

"What did you say?" she asked, still staring at Sorcha.

"You heard right," Sorcha told her, swivelling her gaze to look at her sister. Her eyes were bright with tears. "It's Eoghan's baby."

"Oh, Sorcha."

Ciara was at a complete loss for words. Not just for her sister, but for her parents too who seemed lost and struggling for some way to react. Sorcha gave a small shrug and turned back to the pool, the tears spilling down her face. Ciara turned to her parents, numb with shock, still not finding any words to say, to describe the crowded emotions that were spinning round inside her head. What feeling was strongest? she wondered, unable to grasp some sense from her own thoughts. Grief? Bewilderment? Confusion? Questions kept popping up like masses of bubbles from a drowning person's mouth. When did you find out? How did you find out? What's going to happen? Who knows? How long has Sorcha known? When were you going to tell me? But she couldn't get her lips to form the words because her thoughts were thundering ahead at a hundred miles an hour. There was no way her speech could catch up with them.

So she kept staring at her parents.

And they stared back.

The loudspeaker crackled into life. All qualifiers for the senior girls 400-metres IM finals were to make their way immediately to the deep end of the pool. Sorcha's head jerked round and her eyes met Ciara's.

"That's your race, Ciara," she told her.

"I know."

But she didn't move.

"Go on, Ciara," Sorcha pleaded with her. "Go and swim your race."

"How can I, Sorcha? How can I go now?" All of a sudden, the race seemed trivial and meaningless.

Sorcha didn't answer. Her eyes filled with tears again.

"Go on, Ciara," her father said. "Just do your best."

Ciara looked at him. She glanced at her mother, who smiled again: a too-wide smile. Ciara turned and ran down the steps of the spectator gallery and on to the poolside where she met Mark, who had been waving at her frantically.

"I don't believe that you chose this moment to go and have a chat with your parents!" he spluttered. "Are you trying to give me a heart attack?"

Ciara looked at him.

"Sorry," she muttered. She glanced up to where her family sat. Sorcha gave her a brief wave. "Just had to catch up on a couple of things."

He ushered her over to her diving block, taking her sweatshirt from her as she peeled it off.

Ciara was in lane 5 and she stood behind the block.

"Now remember," Mark told her just before leaving, "focus your thinking and concentrate. Good luck!"

And she was on her own. Except for a million thoughts whirling round her brain.

"Swimmers on the blocks, please."

The voice over the loudspeaker system crackled, silencing the spectators. Ciara took several slow, deep breaths, clearing her mind of everything but the race she was about to swim. Don't think of what has just happened, she told herself. Don't think of what's going to happen. Nothing else is important at this moment but the race. Nothing else is happening right now. You know your form. You know your strategy. Now put it into action. It has to be now.

She stood up on the diving block, curling her toes over the edge, staring down at the clear blue water.

"Take your marks . . ."

Ciara stepped carefully to the edge of the block, getting her balance.

"Get set . . ."

She tensed herself and crouched over.

"Go!"

When the whistle blew to start the race, Ciara launched herself out, stretching towards the water.

The butterfly stroke was first. The first stroke, the first length, the first gauge of her self-control, testing her ability to tighten up her thinking and concentrate.

For now, nothing else mattered.

Chapter 15

Mr Barrett sat at the top of the class and smiled down at the fifth-year students who sat in orderly rows in front of him. They gazed back soberly. It was the beginning of the school year, after all, and sitting listening to him droning on was about as much as they could manage.

"How does it feel to have graduated from transition year and into the serious atmospheric conditions of fifth year?" he asked rhetorically, rubbing his hands together. "The homeward run. The final chapter – the penultimate for a select few of you – in your educational life."

He shifted his gaze to the window, from where the warm rays of the September sun daubed smudges of gold on to the dust motes that hung in the air.

"Ah yes, another batch of fine young men and women preparing for the most significant examination of their lives. A two-year programme of intense study and discovery for all of you." His gaze lingered momentarily on Eoghan, sitting in the front row with his legs cramped beneath him. "Some of you may struggle and fall . . ." Edel Lucas sat next to Eoghan, her eyes bright as she listened intently to the words of the teacher, " . . . while others will coast to victory with ease . . . "

"Who does he think he is?" Mary-Anne whispered to Katie, sitting next to her in the back row. "Bleedin Shakespeare?" She rocked back in her chair, balancing on the two back legs.

Mr Barrett fixed her with a cold eye. "Then again, there are those of you who may not even get as far as the Senior Certificate. You may fall by the wayside like scattered seeds, where you will remain, wasted and shrivelled."

"Some seeds do better in the wayside, sir," piped up Eoghan, who had been listening all along. "Dandelions and cow-parsley and the like grow madly in the ditch. You never see them doing so well in gardens and fields."

Mr Barrett gazed upwards at the ceiling, pausing for a moment before continuing patiently. "Weeds, Eoghan. Those are weeds. That's why they do well, because they continuously choke and smother others who are trying to grow and develop. They deserve the ditch. And they certainly have no place in my classroom."

Eoghan glanced sheepishly at Mr Barrett. "Yessir." Then he slumped down in his chair, counting the minutes until the end of the class.

The first day of the school year was always tedious. Not only did it seem to go on forever, but the teachers never had anything much to say. They could hardly start harping on about homework or chapters to be read or last week's essays. And they were usually disgruntled about being back at school, too, so it was an ordeal all round. This time, in particular, it appeared to be more of a struggle than ever. All Eoghan could think about was the school holidays and the long, warm days, generally spent with Sorcha. The summer had stretched on endlessly, and seemed to be full of laughter and ice cream and holding hands during walks in the park and bags of chips in the snooker hall. Even if his memory was playing sneaky tricks on him, Eoghan didn't mind. There had of course been sour days, with some serious black spots where parents and decision-making and the baby's arrival were concerned. And Sorcha and himself had had their quarrels too. Nothing had been finalised – Eoghan's and Sorcha's parents both decided that it was early days yet and they were too young to make any momentous decisions about their futures. Let things tick over for the time being.

Both Sorcha and Eoghan were to stay on in school as long as reasonably possible and then see after that.

Sorcha had been pretty sick too, but that had settled over time. Once she got through the first couple of months, she'd improved. As she began to feel better, she wanted to spend more time with Eoghan. That suited him fine. They had spent their days outside, strolling around or sitting in the park.

Now it was back to earth with a jolt. During the holidays, school was a million miles away; classrooms and homework a bad dream remembered from a restless night. Study and detention and exams were taboo subjects, horror stories to send a shiver down the spine.

Now Eoghan was in the middle of a waking nightmare.

Not only was he back into the tiresome routine of school, but Sorcha wasn't even there to cheer him up. Mrs Graham, with all her ancient wisdom, had decided that Sorcha should repeat transition year, as her study would be disrupted by hospital visits and the impending arrival of the baby. Then, depending on how everything worked out, she might progress into fifth year the following September.

So instead of Sorcha, Eoghan had the world's greatest study-geek to keep him company: Edel Lucas. Mind you, it was partly his own doing. He had chosen to sit in the front row. Let's face it, anything was better than being stuck next to Mary-Anne at the moment. She wasn't exactly a bundle of laughs since she'd heard about Sorcha's pregnancy. Eoghan thought she was going to have a fit on the spot when he'd told her that Sorcha was expecting his baby. Mary-Anne's face had gone bright purple and her eyes looked like they were going to pop out and roll along the ground as she stared at him like a zombie. Even Katie had been distracted enough to forget Eoghan's news. "Mary-Anne," she'd said, "are you OK? Are you going to collapse?"

It was several moments before Mary-Anne had been able to speak again, and even then, it was hardly a profound statement.

"I think I'm going to throw up," she'd spluttered before rushing off to the toilets in the snooker hall. Katie gave Eoghan a daggers look before following Mary-Anne. When they hadn't reappeared in half an hour, Eoghan decided to make himself scarce and left the snooker hall.

It didn't bode well for the new school year, Eoghan mused.

Ciara, two floors down and facing her first class of the year with Miss Keenan, was feeling decidedly different about progressing into transition year. For a start, she had no serious study pressures or examinations. That meant schoolwork could take a back-seat role this year. And secondly, at the introductory talk about transition year given by Mrs Graham, it had been emphasised that one of the primary aims of transition was for the pupils to discover their achievable vocational goals and to work towards exploring them in greater detail. That was a doddle to Ciara. She knew exactly what her vocational goals were and working on exploring them would be wonderful. It meant she could spend most of the year concentrating on her swimming.

"Isn't this great?" Ciara whispered to Sorcha, sitting beside her on the floor of the gym.

"Marvellous," Sorcha muttered drearily. She was feeling really out of sorts. Being back at school was enough of an ordeal, but being in the same class as her chirpy little sister was a major drag. She was going to go out of her head, she reckoned by, oh, probably next week. Ciara was so perky and full of beans, trotting around like some fruit-loopy head-case so that Sorcha thought she'd end up strangling her.

In addition, having to go through all the same old boring stuff that she'd gone through last year with a complete new batch of students (third group in less than a year) was cracking her up.

And finally, doing it all with a swelling bump in her belly was no joke. She looked down now and adjusted her sweater. She allowed herself a smug little smile.

If anything was going to get her through this year and out the other side with her sanity intact, her baby was. It was the one thing that Sorcha was happy about. Even after the huge rows at home about Eoghan and her, and endless lectures about her stupidity and recklessness, Sorcha still maintained that the baby was something positive. Just about every insult under the sun had been dragged out and thrown at her, and what wasn't said about Eoghan wasn't worth thinking about.

But Sorcha had weathered it, and now she was back

at school and determined to get through, despite all the hassles.

" . . . so we get to do work exploration as a subject!" Ciara told her now, her eyes wide with excitement. "I could find out about professional swimming and getting a US college scholarship, Sorcha."

Sorcha looked at the animated face of her sister and nodded, smiling at her.

Ciara had had a great year, and she deserved it, Sorcha decided. Despite being told shattering news before a major swimming event, she had shown the tenacity and concentration needed to win. Not only had she won in the Leinsters, but Ciara had beaten her own personal best by four seconds. Four hundred-metre IM in four minutes fifty-two seconds – a new Irish record for the distance at senior girls' level.

After that, she had gone on to scoop two golds and a silver at the national championships and had been spotted by a scout from the professional swimming body in the United States. He'd had a long chat with Ciara and her parents and Mark, and had discussed the idea of Ciara going to the States to swim professionally, after her schooling, of course. During the summer, he wanted Ciara to spend two months with his swimming team and she had flown out to California in July. She'd only got back two weeks ago, sunburnt and starry-eyed about American swimming facilities.

Sorcha shook her head. Quite a difference between them, she mused.

"Come on, dreamer," Ciara interrupted Sorcha's thoughts. She was standing beside her, beckoning her. "Don't sit there all day. We've to get the mats out from the store cupboard."

"Not me," Sorcha replied, smiling. "I've strict instructions to take it easy. I'm staying right where I am!"